Enc

By

Kate Rudolph
and Starr Huntress

More by Kate Rudolph

Soulless

Ruthless

Heartless

Faultless

Chapter One

A heavy weight pressed down on Dryce's chest, a cold, unfeeling dread that unfurled and tried to settle over his exposed skin. The black expanse of space stretched out beyond his eyes, silver dots in the distance the only relief from an eternity of darkness. It was all that was left for him, no matter how the week ended. He could feel the certainty of his fate just as surely as a wave crashing onto the shore.

War was coming, and with it the same weapon that had destroyed his home planet generations before he was born. He and his fellow warriors had summoned it to Earth where they would doom billions if they couldn't find a way to stop it.

And even if they did, Dryce was just as damned as he'd been before he fled Detyen Headquarters with his brother. Soon he would die, or worse, and though the men around him had all found their denyai, Dryce couldn't believe that one would be out there for him. On the eve of war, he wouldn't waste his luck on such a wish.

His eyes snapped open and Dryce eyed the clock on his bedside table. It wasn't even midnight. He could hear muffled laughter from one room over and knew that Kayde and his denya, Quinn, had yet to find their sleep. Toran and his denya were likely to be at her house and Raze rarely spent time in the suite of rooms that they'd all been assigned when they made it to the planet. As for the final pair in the group, Dryce didn't know where Druath and Laurel were sleeping tonight, but after what had just happened to Laurel, Dryce knew the two of them would want to capture some time alone while they could manage it.

He ran his fingers through his short dark hair and groaned. Sleep eluded him, just as it had so many nights since he'd first come to Earth. The place was so *loud* and bright, and nothing ever slowed down to a manageable speed. He'd seen dozens of planets and hundreds of cities, some far more technologically advanced than Washington, DC, but something about this city caused his heart to beat a little faster.

He threw the covers off his bed and sat up. Dryce could lay down for the next four hours, but he knew that sleep wouldn't come without something to aid it along. And while there were plenty of medicinal sleep aids available to him, he'd found only one solution that led to a good night's rest and a happy mood in the morning.

Dark pants, tight shirt, and a comb through his hair was all that it took to get him ready. He stepped out of his room and walked quietly through the common area so as not to disturb any of his flat mates. He called up a taxi on his communicator and by the time he made it downstairs it was already waiting. He put in the address for a nearby bar and watched the streetlights fly by as they cut through the scant traffic of DC late at night. He'd always enjoyed a few hours with a willing and exuberant body, and on Earth he'd found a level of popularity he'd never dreamed of. The people at the clubs and bars here loved a bit of alien flesh, and he was more than willing to oblige in the no-strings-attached encounters.

It was a little hollow, a little lonely, even in the hot crowds, but Dryce could deal with that, especially when finding a willing partner would give him what he needed for the night.

He paid the taxi and watched it drive away. A line snaked around the side of the building, but when the bouncer spotted him, he waved Dryce right in. It was good to be known, and the smile he offered those waiting outside seemed to go a long way to soothe their ruffled tempers.

Inside, music blasted, and bodies writhed on the dance floor. Dryce slithered and gyrated his way to the nearest bar and ordered a drink, nothing too hard, nothing that he would regret in the morning, but he found he liked the taste of Earth beers and despite his teal skin and occasionally red eyes, holding a bottle made him fit in among all of these strange beige and brown people. There weren't just humans in the room. He spotted a dozen or so aliens, some bright blue and one with tentacles for arms. He'd keep his distance from that group. It was easier to prowl for a partner alone than pick off a hanger-on from the alien groupies.

And he'd been coming here enough to have groupies of his own.

"Dryce! I didn't think you were coming tonight." He could hear the smile in her voice even before he turned around. Renee was a short human who he'd met at several of the bars in the city, though they'd never gone home together. She was eternally cheerful and welcoming, offering him a hug whenever they met and introducing him to whatever friends she had with her. He'd picked up plenty of the friends, but something about Renee made her feel more like a younger sister than a potential lover.

He smiled and returned her hug. "You know me, I can't stay away."

She giggled, but they both knew how true it was. When his duties didn't keep him overnight, more often than not he was out. His fellow warriors were content to stay at home, and lucky to have their denyai by their sides, but he had to find his comforts elsewhere.

"You should meet my friend Ella, she's never been here, but she *loves* you already. Come on!" Renee tugged on his arm and pulled him towards the corner of the room where the mysterious Ella was waiting. Dryce didn't know if she already loved him specifically because

Renee had been talking about him, or if the woman was looking for a bit of alien fun, but either way worked. If they clicked, he could show her a good time and they'd both leave pleased.

Maybe she'd even be his mate.

The hope barely had time to form before it was dashed by the sight of a beautiful young woman who waved when Renee came into sight. She was short, with long dark hair and skin that seemed to sit between pale beige and something more golden. And she wasn't his denya. Dryce didn't know what it would feel like to find his mate, but he knew he'd recognize it immediately. Raze had tried to explain it to him but given that his brother had been soulless at the time he met his own denya, his experience wasn't likely to match what Dryce would feel if the moment ever came.

He talked to the women for a few minutes, but whatever charms Ella possessed weren't what he was looking for that night. He excused himself, pretending to see another person he knew, and left the two women alone to continue their evening. For a second Ella seemed disappointed, but she barely pouted as he moved away.

He surveyed the room, looking for someone who would do as his companion. Plenty of patrons eyed him, making it clear they'd love to show him a good time, but none of it felt right. He clunked his head back against the wall in frustration. It looked like it was going to be another long, sleepless night. Dryce checked his watch and saw that it had only ticked by midnight. He hadn't even been gone from his room for an hour, but he was ready to head back. Given the mood he was in, he doubted he'd find someone who could satisfy him. And given his own grouchiness, he didn't trust that he would be the best partner for a potential lover tonight.

He turned to walk away and recognition lit through him, despite the dim light and the crowd.

Denya.

Dryce pushed himself off the wall and dove through the crowd, no longer caring if he jostled anyone. He gently hip checked someone who wouldn't move out of his way and heard a cry as a drink spilled to the ground. He didn't care. His entire focus was on the woman standing haloed in the light of the door. She was looking for someone, her eyes narrowed and lips scowling, clearly not happy to be there.

But how would she feel when she saw him? Would she recognize him? Could he take her home now and claim her tonight?

His heart beat faster than it did in the heat of battle as hope surged through him. His mate! She was here! He just had to get to her. All thoughts of finding another lover *ever* dissolved as he imagined what it would be like with her. He had to get to her. Had to find out her name, where she lived, when she would want him, what he could do to prove himself to her. He knew that humans didn't always understand the denya bond. Detyens mating with humans was still new, but he would find a way to make this work, and he'd do it much more smoothly than his fellow warriors had.

Raze and Kayde, due to their soulless natures, hadn't even recognized their mates when they'd first met.

Toran and Iris had been at odds due to Iris's job and the human's initial distrust of the Detyens. And Dru and Laurel had famously clashed before they mated.

He wasn't going to suffer like that. He'd find his mate and woo her, prove to her that he was just the man for her, and then she'd be his, sated and safely ensconced beside him.

She pulled out a communicator and the light caught a bright sticker on the back of it. He couldn't quite make it out, but that didn't matter. A moment later the communicator disappeared from her hand as she put it away. She gave the room a final survey and huffed out a breath before turning around and making for the door.

She hadn't spared him a single glance.

Dryce redoubled his efforts to get through the crowd, which seemed somehow even thicker the closer he got to the door. He made it to the spot where she'd been standing and thought he might have caught a hint of a floral perfume, something she'd been wearing. And on the ground lay a communicator with a bright reflective sticker of a smiling face.

His denya's communicator.

His head shot up and he saw her duck through the door. He sprinted after her, but by the time he got outside, she was nowhere to be seen. He turned to the bouncer, but the man was caught up in an intense conversation with two patrons and didn't seem to be paying any mind to the street.

His denya was gone. And he didn't know anything about her.

Her communicator beeped and a message flashed up on the screen. And almost in time with the notification, Dryce had an idea. A slide of his finger lit the device up, and quick navigation brought him to her contact list. He had one way to find her, and he'd do whatever it took to make sure she became his.

***

Peyton Cho made it all the way back to her apartment before she realized her communicator wasn't in her pocket. She groaned and slumped back against the door as her options flashed through her head. She could go back out, take the two busses back to the bar, pray that no one creepy was on board, hope that no one had stolen it, talk to the bartender and hope someone had turned the thing in, and then get back on the bus and hope again that she avoided the creeps.

Or she could tear off her dirty clothes and collapse into her bed and save that problem for the morning.

Ignoring her problems won, but when she woke up she could smell the faint scent of beer permeating the clothes she hadn't managed to struggle out of before sleep claimed her, and that smell had sunk into her sheets.

"Ella, I'm going to kill you." She muttered it into her pillow and tried to bargain with herself to claim a few more minutes of slumber. But her clock told her it was almost time to wake up anyway, and seeing as she was down a communicator, she'd nccd to fit time in her schedule to head back to that bar and hope someone had turned the thing in.

Ugh, she couldn't even make it through her shower before her problems started to catch up to her.

She heard tinkering in the kitchen and let out a relieved breath. Only a few people knew the code to get into her apartment, and only one of those people lived with her. Well, *supposedly* lived with her. It seemed like Ella was away more nights than she was there. Peyton tried to remind herself that she wasn't her sister's babysitter, but old habits died hard, and the city could be dangerous for a girl like Ella. There'd been plenty of stories of young women being snatched off the street and abducted by slavers who took them to far away planets and sold them as slaves.

At first, Peyton had been sure that the stories were exaggerations. But after news had broken a few months ago of nearly a dozen women who'd been returned to Earth after their abductions, she'd grown worried. And she'd started to request that Ella check in with her if she was going to stay the night out. She didn't see how it was such a big ask to know that her sister was safe, but Ella acted like Peyton was her warden, and recently she'd been sneaking away more and more.

That was how Peyton ended up at a crowded bar on a Wednesday night. She'd heard that Ella was there and just wanted to check on her. She'd seen nothing of her sister and had only managed to lose her communicator. But if Ella was back now, maybe she could breathe easy.

Yeah, right.

She'd relax when her sister started to realize that the world actually *could* be dangerous, and she accepted that a few damn precautions weren't the end of the world.

Peyton pushed herself out of bed and into the bathroom. The shower woke her up a little, and by the time she was in the kitchen, Ella had the coffee made and was working on breakfast as she hummed a tune that Peyton didn't recognize.

"When did you get in?" she asked as mildly as she could manage. "I didn't realize you were coming home last night."

Ella offered her a bright smile, as if she didn't realize how close her sister was to wringing her neck. "Two or something? Renee introduced me to some great people, but none of us clicked. I hope this one alien comes back. He was *so* hot. I think if we hang out a little more…"

Peyton clenched her hands around her almost too hot coffee mug and tuned her sister out. If she hadn't come home until two, that meant she was barely working on four hours of sleep, and yet she looked more rested than Peyton. Stress was a motherfucker.

"You're not upset, are you?" Ella finally wound down her recounting of events and her lips curved into a hopeful smile.

Peyton's anger fled. It had just been the two of them for so long that she never managed to stay angry long, especially not once she knew Ella was home safe. The girl had the defensive instincts of a leaf, but she was kind and young and just wanted to have fun. And it wasn't like she'd ever gotten herself into any danger, at least not any that Peyton knew about. And Ella didn't keep secrets.

Peyton opened her arms and Ella rushed her, enveloping her in a tight hug that smelled of the sweet shampoo she used. "I'm not angry," she assured her. "I just wish you'd remember to contact me like I asked."

Ella pulled back and her face took on an uncharacteristically mulish expression. "I *did*. Last night I texted you and told you I was coming back, but *you* didn't respond."

Peyton looked away and felt her cheeks heat. "I'm sorry. I didn't check my communicator. I must have already been asleep." She didn't want her sister to know that she'd tried to hunt her down; that was guaranteed to lead to an argument and both of them had work to get to.

And just like always, Ella's negative feelings evaporated. She wasn't made to hold anger in. She kissed Peyton's cheek and retreated to her room to get ready for the day, leaving Peyton with her thoughts and a cooling breakfast.

She felt naked without her communicator as she climbed aboard the bus to head in to work, and the entire morning she hoped that no one tried to contact her using her normal number, at least not with anything important.

She used her office communicator to call the bar around lunch time and almost promised her first born child to the person who answered when they confirmed that a communicator that looked like hers had been left with the bartender the night before. She ducked out of the office to get a sandwich and sprang for a taxi to get to the bar before she had to be back to continue with her duties. Things had been speeding up on a variety of projects over the last month and they were finally coming to a head. Peyton couldn't afford to miss out.

It was a simple matter of getting the device back when she showed up to the bar and then she was on her way back to work, clutching the communicator to her chest and seriously considering one of the implanted models. She couldn't loser her comm if it was attached to her.

But those had a bad habit of shorting out and burning their users, and she'd never been a fan of pain.

Half a dozen messages were waiting for her when she started to scroll through, but nothing too important. And just like Ella had said, she'd contacted Peyton and told her she was coming home.

Right under that message was one from a contact she didn't recognize. She scrunched her brows together as she racked her brain to think of who DF could be, but she couldn't figure it out. When she read the message, she realized it was whoever had recovered her phone. Apparently he'd added himself to her contacts and left her a text. She almost deleted it on principle; she wasn't about to flirt with some guy who went to that kind of bar on a Wednesday night, but on the other hand, he'd been kind enough to turn in her comm and she'd be helpless without it. The least she could do was respond.

Once.

DF: Sorry I couldn't return this in person. I saw you across the room and it shined.

Peyton rolled her eyes. Did lines like that actually *work* on people?

Peyton: Thanks for turning it in. You're a life saver. :)

There. Simple, thankful, done. She put thoughts of DF and Ella out of her mind as her bus pulled up in front of her office. Rumors of a big assignment going out had been running rampant, and she needed to have her head in the game if she was going to be the one chosen. Her comm beeped again with an incoming message, but Peyton ignored it. She had work to do.

The incoming alien fleet wasn't going to defeat itself.

Chapter Two

Dryce stared at his comm waiting for Peyton to reply to his message. It felt almost intrusive to know her name, but the info had been right there in her contacts. She'd thanked him, so he knew she'd retrieved her comm from the bar, but after he replied to her, she hadn't said anything. And as the minutes ticked by he feared that she wouldn't reply again. He wanted to prompt her, but he knew enough about flirtation to know that no person liked to be hounded for a response.

He shoved the comm back in his pocket as Sandon opened the door to the small conference room they were meeting in and took a seat. "I've sent a list of interviews you've been scheduled for to your communicator. They will be happening over today and tomorrow. We're getting reports of amateur detection of the fleet at the edge of the solar system and our joint leadership team does not want to incite panic. Do you understand?"

Dryce understood that he was stuck in a job he had no skill for just because he had a pretty face and an easy smile. He was a warrior, not a puppet, but for some reason both the SDA and Detyen leadership had decided he was the perfect person to liaise with the media about the Detyen presence on Earth.

"Sir, is this—"

"I wouldn't assign it to you if it wasn't necessary, would I?" Sandon didn't let him get the question out. It was times like this that Dryce remembered Sandon wasn't that much older than him. He wasn't yet thirty, though the day was drawing close. Soon the commander would need to make a decision, whether he would die or sacrifice all of his emotions to buy a few more years in service of his people. The stress of the past months was wearing on the man, and from the pinched look on his face, he seemed to be living with a constant headache. Dryce could add to the man's problems by rebelling at his assignment, or he could do his duty to his people, no matter how unpleasant it seemed.

"I'll keep news of the fleet out of the interviews," Dryce promised. "But do we have any updates on that?"

Sandon shook his head. "They're holding steady on this side of the Kuiper belt." Dryce had learned that the Kuiper belt delineated the outer edge of the main Sol system. The system continued on for a long distance past that, but it was mostly uninhabitable rocks and radiation. "No matter who questions Brakley Varrow, he won't give up any information. The Oscavian we captured with him is just as reluctant to divulge their secrets."

That was beyond frustrating. Brakley Varrow was an Oscavian scientist who had held Dryce's fellow warrior Dru as a captive for months aboard an Oscavian scientific vessel. He'd also experimented on a human woman named Laurel who had turned out to be Dru's denya. The pair had managed to escape Varrow, but in doing so had led him and his allies to the Detyen headquarters. The Detyens had been forced to evacuate and destroy their former home before it could fall into the wrong hands. Dryce hadn't been there, having arrived on Earth months before his fellow Detyens, but everyone in the Legion had a different version of the story to tell.

"Have we heard anything about Yormas of Wreet?" Dryce asked.

"His people claim he's been stripped of his ambassadorship and that any action he takes is on his own, not in any capacity as a Wreetan official." Sandon's droll tone told Dryce all he needed to know. Wreet may have disavowed the man, but they wouldn't lift a finger to stop him from destroying Earth.

For more than a hundred years, the mystery of who had destroyed Detya had haunted the Detyen Legion. A single ship had managed to rain down fire and death and only those lucky enough to already be off planet, or within close proximity to escape ships, had managed to survive. In the century since, the Detyens had cobbled together a culture across the stars, but there'd been no clue as to who had destroyed them or why. No clue until a team of warriors had been sent to a desolate place called Fenryr 1 where they discovered a recording that implicated Yormas of Wreet and promised to let the Detyen Legion fulfill their true purpose.

It was there that Dryce's brother, Raze, had met his own denya, and at the time that had been impossible. Raze had been soulless, had sacrificed his emotions to extend his life beyond the thirty years an unmated Detyen could live. Somehow he'd recognized Sierra Alvarez as his and the next time Dryce had seen him, he'd been a changed man.

So much had changed in less than half a year, but now the Legion was in more trouble than ever, and full of more hope than they could have dreamed. If they could defeat Yormas of Wreet and his allied Oscavians, they could finally have their justice for what was done to their ancestors. And once that was over, perhaps they could grow beyond their original mission and find a home for their people on Earth where it seemed that Detyens were finding denyai by the day.

Dryce included. He couldn't help but smile as he remembered the sight of Peyton. Maybe he should have felt guilty for stealing her name from her communicator and taking her number for himself, but all was fair when it came to claiming a mate, and he would show her he was a worthy companion, just as soon as he could convince her to text him again.

"What's that look?" Sandon asked, jerking him out of his memory.

Dryce schooled his expression into something more serious. "Nothing, sir. Thank you for the update. I'll complete the interviews and make sure not to shirk my training."

Sandon nodded. "See to it." He glanced down at his watch and grimaced before shaking his head. "I think I'm wishing for an attack just so I can avoid all of these meetings."

There was the Sandon Dryce had once known, before the weight of leadership had overwhelmed him. "Don't pray too hard, or our ancestors might do you a favor."

The commander gave a short laugh as he pushed himself up from his chair and left Dryce alone. Dryce pulled out his own communicator to find the schedule of interviews that Sandon had left for him. They were scheduled throughout the next two days, but luckily he'd be able to do them all from SDA headquarters. He'd been forced to do a few in front of media cameras in studio and that had eaten into most of his time. He was a warrior, not a decoration, and he didn't want to spend his days smiling for the media and assuring the public that there was no incoming threat. Especially when he knew that threat was waiting for them to show a single sign of weakness.

His communicator beeped and a message from Peyton flashed up.

Dryce: Sometimes I wish I could throw my comm away, but I'm glad you have yours back.

Peyton: Too many of your conquests trying to get ahold of you?

Her response startled a laugh out of him and he couldn't stop grinning. Maybe another man would have been rebuffed, but he liked that his mate had claws of her own.

Dryce: Do you think I give my conquests my contact info?

He sent the response before he could think better of it and as soon as he realized what he'd typed he winced and wished he could call it back. That was no way to ingratiate himself with his mate. She should never have to doubt her place beside him, and his days of picking up people in bars and clubs were past now that he'd found her. Even if she never wanted him, he didn't think he could take someone else to his bed; he wouldn't even want to try.

Despite his inelegant message, she replied almost immediately.

Peyton: So what makes me so spccial? Or is it because you don't want to make me one of your conquests?

His fingers itched to tap out a message, but he forced himself to slow down, to think before he replied. If he told her too much too soon, he risked scaring her away before she could accept what she already meant to him. If he made light of how he'd been on the planet up to this point, she might never take him seriously as a romantic partner.

Dryce: I needed to make sure you got your comm back. It's more important than a blaster on Earth.

Peyton: You're right about that.

She left it there without another response, but Dryce smiled down at the message history before flicking back to his schedule. It wasn't much of a conversation, but it was a beginning. Now he just had to stop the world from ending to make sure that it could continue.

***

"Why are the Oscavians so fucking formal?" Jessa Stewart slumped against Peyton's door as she lobbed her complaint into the air.

Peyton looked up from her communicator, hoping her dark hair hid her blush. She wasn't supposed to be using the device for non-work purposes, and messaging DF surely couldn't count as official business. "Oscavians?" she asked. "Since when do we care about Oscavians?" The empire was on the other side of the galaxy, and though its tendrils spread every day, Earth was in no danger of falling under its dominion. They were too far away and too insignificant to matter to such a powerful nation.

Jessa stepped forward and melted into the other chair in Peyton's office. Well, the office Peyton had claimed for the day. She was normally down in the lab dissecting alien tech, but today several of their new alien allies had taken over and kicked her out, so she was stuck looking at teleporter schematics on a borrowed computer and filing paperwork that she'd let get backed up.

"We care because a bunch of them are sitting in space a bit too close to home."

The hairs on the back of Peyton's neck stood up at that. Whispers had been snaking their way through the SDA research labs for the past several weeks, but as far as she could tell, all information was on a strictly need to know basis. And Peyton hadn't needed to know. But Jessa wasn't likely to let something as silly as rules about classified information keep her from complaining. "How close?" Peyton asked. It was one thing to worry about nefarious aliens kidnapping her sister off the streets. Even at her most paranoid, she knew it wasn't that likely to happen. An actual interstellar army sitting at their doorstep was another matter.

"Close enough for civilians to pick them up. I hear our new alien friends are going to run interference with Star Hottie, but I don't think that will work for long." Jessa leaned forward and picked up a paperweight that sat at the edge of the desk and tossed it from hand to hand.

"Don't break shit that isn't mine," Peyton begged. And then her mind caught up to the rest of what Jessa had said. "Wait, who's Star Hottie?"

"That hot alien guy that's done all the interviews over the past few weeks? Haven't you watched?" Jessa was another woman completely obsessed with their new interstellar friends.

Peyton didn't get it. Sure it was kind of fascinating to think about all of the things the Detyens and the other aliens who'd come to Earth had seen, but that didn't make her want to run out and climb on the dick of the nearest eligible alien. Did they even have dicks? She bit her tongue to keep from asking. "You're talking about the Detyen media liaison?" Yeah, even Peyton could admit he was hot, maybe a little *too* hot, but she didn't want to tell that to Jessa.

Jessa's eyes brightened. "Any chance I get I'm talking about him. I've been praying every day that he gets assigned to our team for something."

"Somehow I doubt that's going to happen." She and Jessa worked for the SDA, but they were both science grunts. Peyton spent most of her days tearing apart scavenged alien tech and trying to rebuild it for use on Earth. Jessa was a report writing machine. She could translate all of the science crap—Jessa's words—to something that the higher ups understood. Her memos had been singlehandedly responsible for expanding the entire department's budget on more than one occasion, something she didn't let their supervisors forget when it came time for annual raises. "How did you hear about the Oscavians?"

Of the many aliens on Earth, Peyton didn't think she'd ever met an Oscavian. They were mostly characters in stories, used in media shows as distant princes or evil villains bent on galactic domination. She'd heard rumors that one was being held captive on an SDA base, but even that seemed farfetched. Though if Jessa's gossip was true, maybe the other rumors were as well.

"I have my sources." Jessa grinned.

Peyton's communicator beeped and she could feel herself blush. God, barely a few lines of text flirting and her heart went pitter-patter. How pathetic was that? She reached out and tried to casually cover the device so that Jessa couldn't reach for it, but that somehow brought more attention to it.

"What's that?" Jessa asked. "Who's messaging you?"

"I didn't look, so how could I know?" Peyton shot back. It had been a weird night and day, and her thoughts were all jumbled up, that was all. No reason to get tripped up over the mysterious DF.

"I don't think I've ever seen you blush." Jessa leaned forward and reached out for the hand covering Peyton's comm. Peyton yanked it back and stuck it in her pocket before it could be stolen. "And you're not usually so possessive. Come on. Spill! I don't give a shit about our imminent destruction if you've got something fun to share."

Peyton weighed her options. No way was Jessa walking out of this office without *something*, well, not unless there was a fire drill. But the alarm trigger was down the hall, so that option was out. She didn't know why she was so reluctant to share. It was just some harmless messages. But there was something about them that she wanted to hold close, to keep to herself for a little longer. Ugh, maybe she just needed to get laid. It had been too long and if she was mooning over a mystery man, a man whose name and face she didn't know, she definitely needed to get out more.

And as it always went, Peyton relented. "I lost my comm last night." No need to admit she'd been trailing her sister to make sure she didn't do anything too stupid. "And this guy turned it in. When I picked it up this morning, we started chatting. It's nothing. He seems nice."

"Nice?" Jessa practically jumped up in her chair. "What's his name? Is he cute? Is he single?"

"I don't know!" Peyton clutched her comm tight to her chest and squeezed, as if she could pry information out of it. "I'm sure it will end up being nothing, but it's a nice distraction. Seeing as you're telling me about the potential *end of the world*!"

Jessa rolled her eyes. "Shut up, you're fine. And if it is the end of the world, maybe you should see where things with your mystery man go. If we're all about to die fiery deaths, you have literally nothing left to lose." She checked her watch and heaved a sigh before pushing up from her seat. "Duty calls. I'm going to want a full report on how things go."

Petyon shook her head. "Yes, boss, I'll get right on that." But as soon as Jessa was gone, she glanced down at the screen and couldn't help her grin at the message waiting from DF.

DF: You took off quick last night. Next time you should let me buy you a drink.

Maybe next time she would.

Chapter Three

Peyton: I can be pretty picky about my drinks. Do you think you're up for it?

Dryce grinned as he slipped his comm into his pocket. He wanted to reply, but he had to get to the third floor to start his first interview of the day and if Sandon heard he was late there would be hell to pay. Once he was situated in a different conference room he read through all of the information that the Detyens and the SDA wanted to get out to the public. Most of it was a bid to reassure everyone that the Detyens had come to Earth seeking shelter and new lives and that they meant the humans no harm. And when he was asked about the fleet just waiting to attack them, he knew what he'd have to do.

But the interview went smoothly enough. Dryce flirted with the woman who'd been sent to interview him, charming her just as he charmed everyone. It went so well that she almost forgot to ask him about the imminent threat, but as they got to the end of the interview, he realized that it was possibly him who'd been lulled into a false sense of complacency.

"Is this Oscavian Empire responsible for the fleet of ships waiting at the edge of our solar system?" The reporter, Holly Fordham, asked so casually that Dryce almost answered without thought.

Almost. He took a moment and kept his smile in place. "The Oscavian Empire?" He laughed. "I may be new to Earth, but last I heard, they had no reason to want anything from this planet or system. If any Oscavians are here, I'm sure they just want to see the sights."

"And the fleet amassing in our system?" Holly pressed.

"Ships come and go every day, Holly." Though his job was to redirect attention, he'd been cautioned to lie as little as possible. And Dryce knew that outright denying a fleet sitting somewhere in the solar system would only draw attention to it. He didn't want more amateur astronomers pointing their telescopes taking a peek. But he could see that she was gearing up to press him further, so he kept talking. "My people are warriors, so we've dedicated our entire existence to the protection of our people, and now that Earth is our home, our protection extends here. If there were any sort of threat, we would be first in line to fight it. Earth is safe, and I will give my last breath defending it."

Her eyes narrowed ever so slightly, but she wrapped up the interview with a few more easy questions before the media units turned off. "So what's the real story about those ships?" she asked, her posture sagging slightly and the tight smile dropping off her face.

Dryce just looked at her. Another part of his training had told him that reporters could be more effective than spies at ferreting out information. Even if they were no longer being recorded, it didn't mean she wouldn't use everything he told her. "I hope the drive here was pleasant. I know it's a bit out of the way."

Holly sighed, but gave up her pursuit. They chatted for a few minutes while her people cleaned up before leaving Dryce alone. Only once she was gone did he realize that he hadn't flirted with her beyond what was needed to get the job done. It had come naturally before, and more than one reporter and crewmember were among his conquests. But not even for a second had he looked at Holly as anything but an adversarial emissary. She wanted information he couldn't give, but he needed to use her to calm the populace. Whether she'd make a good bed partner hadn't flitted across his mind.

Of course, even at his most promiscuous, Dryce hadn't flirted with *everybody*. And before seeing Peyton, it was completely possible that he would not have tried to make a move on Holly. She was too sharp eyed to let his guard down around, even if only in joining their bodies together.

He'd heard that the denya bond was powerful. But even when he contemplated it, he'd wondered if it was powerful enough to override his normally voracious appetite. And he'd wondered if he would miss it. Though it hadn't even been a full day yet, he couldn't say that he did. He only wanted to find a way to meet with Peyton and woo her to his side and his bed.

He grabbed his comm since he had a few minutes between meetings and frowned at the message she sent.

Peyton: I don't think I trust that pretty boy.

DF: Pretty boy?

A lick of jealousy lashed him, something so unfamiliar to Dryce that it took him a moment to figure out what it actually was. Who was she looking at? Why was he pretty? But then as he realized what she was actually saying, a sense of satisfaction suffused him. Whoever this guy was, she didn't respect him or want to be near him. He wasn't competition for Dryce.

Peyton: That alien that they keep interviewing. He's so slick and charming that you just know he's hiding something.

Dryce stared at his comm for a full minute as the words sank in. *He* was the pretty boy she didn't respect. At least she thought he was charming? Not even that could soften the blow. A cold chasm threatened to open up in his chest at his mate's rejection. A better man than him might have admitted who he was in that moment. He'd known that Peyton couldn't know him, but hadn't realized she might have seen him before, might have formed an opinion about him. And a poor one at that. There was only one solution.

He had to show her that he was more than a pretty face, more than slick charm. And he couldn't let her know who he was just yet, not until she started to think better of him. He wondered if he should ask his fellow warriors for advice. They'd successfully claimed their mates in the last months, and some of them had endured contentious relationships before that. But he could already imagine Raze telling him that his only option was to be honest and show his mate just how faithful and true he could be.

But Dryce had no plans to lie. Not completely. They just weren't going to talk about who he was until it was a bit more… convenient.

DF: I didn't see the interview. We didn't have media like that where I'm from. It was very isolated.

Peyton: Where's that?

DF: An icy planet a long way from here.

Peyton: So you're an alien? I didn't realize that.

DF: Alien is a bit generic. I'm Detyen. You might have heard of us.

Peyton: Really?! Please don't tell me that you know that guy, that I insulted your brother or something!

Along with her message she sent an animation of a small fluffy animal with huge eyes trying to hide itself behind its paws.

DF: Haha! My brother would have laughed at your message. He's said much worse.

Peyton: Older or younger?

DF: He's older by five years. We haven't been close for a long time, but things have recently changed.

Peyton: I'm the older one. Ella is six years younger than me, but sometimes it feels like a century. She's why I was at that bar.

Was her Ella the same one he'd been introduced to? Though the bond had sparked, he hadn't managed a very close look at Peyton, but even from a distance they had the same dark hair and similar skin tone. But so many humans looked alike that it was often hard for Dryce to tell the ones he didn't know apart. Then again, he was sure that many would say the same about the Detyens.

Peyton: I get worried. You hear all these stories about bad things happuring, people getting abducted. Sometimes I think that if she's out of my sight, she has no protection.

A beat passed while Dryce tried to formulate a response, but Peyton wasn't done.

Peyton: I don't know why I'm telling you this. Maybe it's easier because I don't know who you are.

DF: I will keep your secrets. Speak as much as you like.

But the next interviewer was already setting up and Peyton seemed to have work of her own. Despite the hiccup of her initial distrust, Dryce's soul was light. He'd had a real conversation with his mate, and he knew more about her than he could have hoped to learn from a single glance. And soon enough he'd find a way to meet her in person. Even on the brink of battle, even with the Oscavians and Wreetans threatening their very existence, he felt happy, hopeful. He'd find a way to claim Peyton, and they'd beat the bad guys. But first he had to face the media.

***

Peyton spent the next two days sending messages back and forth with her mystery alien. She still didn't know his real name, and after more than a hundred messages exchanged it felt a little late to ask. And a part of her didn't want to. The more anonymous he remained, the easier it was to tell him anything. And a part of her thrilled when she saw the Detyens coming through the building now. Could one of them be her DF? She still blushed to think that she'd accidentally insulted his associate in one of their earlier messages, but they didn't discuss him much further than that.

And maybe Peyton had shied away from that topic. She hadn't been lying when she called Dryce NaFeen, or Star Hottie as Jessa called him, a pretty boy, though if she were being honest, she knew he was all man. The media lights made his teal skin glow greener than she thought possible, and his dark eyes might have held the depths of the universe in them. The first time she'd caught him on an interview, she hadn't heard a word he'd said, so enthralled by the look of him. He was made of muscle and self-assurance, a man who knew just how attractive he was and wasn't afraid to use his charms to get what he wanted.

Yes, he was hot. But Peyton knew plenty of hot human guys, and any of them as hot as Dryce NaFeen were way too conceited for any normal person to deal with. And her own correspondent hadn't exactly leapt to the guy's defense. She didn't normally feel so strongly about strangers, but there was just something about that guy that roused something in her. Something dark and old, something she didn't want to look at too closely for fear that it might be far deeper than she could understand.

She put thoughts of DF and NaFeen out of her mind. The Detyens and the SDA leadership had finally finished with her lab and she was back with hundreds of new goodies to look at. They'd scavenged them all from a speeder from an Oscavian who had tried to abduct a human woman. He was somehow involved in the conflict that she wasn't supposed to know about, and she'd been told that anything she discovered among his things could be necessary for the continued defense of Earth. And she'd been given three days. Three days, four assistants, and hundreds of parts to pore over. A robot couldn't have done it, and she didn't know how she and her team were going to manage a third of the project. But General Remington Alvarez himself had given her the task, and she wouldn't fail.

She gathered Gordon, Fiona, Lilah, and Betty at the main table and took a deep breath. "You've all heard the rumors, right?" News traveled fast, especially among the assistants. Whatever she didn't know, she was sure her minions did.

They all nodded and Peyton didn't bother to ask what exactly those rumors entailed. Her kids understood that this was dire. "We don't know exactly what's coming, but it's going to be bad. Things don't move this fast around here unless the threat is on our doorstep. And given how hard they've been denying that anything's wrong, I think we know that things could go belly up at any moment. Each of you needs to take one of the tables. I want you cataloging thoroughly and quickly. If you think something is unimportant, put it aside. The General thinks his team missed things, which is why it's our turn now. We're going to be here for a few days. If you're not sleeping or eating, you're here. Any objections?"

Her team shook their heads, all of them looking determined to do the job they'd been given. In two days they'd look exhausted, but right now they were ready to dive in.

"Let's get to it."

Her comm beeped and Peyton almost reached for it. She realized she hadn't told DF that she'd be busy for so long, but she didn't owe him the communication, no matter how much she liked it, and she couldn't set a bad example by getting distracted before things had already begun. If anyone official needed to get ahold of her, they'd use the SDA comms that were built into the building. She turned off her personal comm without checking the message and stowed it in her desk. Then she got to work.

The hours melted away as she examined all of the tiny pieces of tech that had been stripped from the Oscavian ship. Though the designs weren't common on Earth, the Oscavian Empire was so influential that she'd easily been able to study their schematics from records available. Everything she studied in front of her lined up with what she'd expected to see. There were a few obvious modifications, but most of the devices and tech they encountered had been mass produced by Oscavians and were available for sale from most shipyards and tech shops.

An official Oscavian military vessel would have had much more advanced tech. Instead of military grade security, she encountered only the barest encryption when she looked at the nav and records systems. It didn't appear that the SDA had ripped through the system, though she was sure they'd grabbed as much information as possible. The man who had commissioned the ship had to have been incredibly ignorant of standard security practices, or he was so arrogant that he didn't believe his ship could fall into enemy hands.

His loss was her gain.

She pulled the logs and fed them into the system, but didn't try to decipher them; that was for the computer techs, not her. She dealt with the physical. And when her physical body started to protest the hunch she'd been sporting for several hours she straightened and couldn't quite suppress a groan. It hurt to stand up and stretch, which was a sure sign that she'd been in one position for far too long.

Peyton looked down the table and almost slumped in defeat. She'd been sure that she'd cataloged enough to make a dent in the daunting number of items she had to work with, but after hours she'd barely passed two dozen. A glance at her fellow scientists showed that none of them were faring much better. Still, she reassured herself, they weren't even through the first day of work. If they just kept going they would get it done.

Something beeped and Lilah jumped up as if she'd been bitten, the movement enough to draw the attention of everyone in the room. Her eyes scrunched together as she held up a small cylinder and examined it closely. She reached for a sensor and started to scan it and when the device continued to beep and blink madly, the look of determination on Lilah's face could have turned a man to stone. Several minutes passed and Peyton wanted to offer assistance, but she feared that breaking Lilah's concentration might set her even farther back. Finally the beeping and blinking subsided and Lilah slumped back, smiling. She looked over at Peyton and raised up the cylinder in her hand. "I think I've found something."

Chapter Four

Sweat dripped from pores that Dryce hadn't known could sweat as his breath heaved and he swung wildly, trying to land a hit against one of his attackers. He was half pinned and flailing to stop his closest opponent from getting a good hold, but that meant he couldn't do much to ward off his other attacker. He'd started in a bad position, not as ready for the fight as he should have been, and he'd fallen to the ground in an embarrassingly short amount of time. But he wasn't about to give up. Detyen warriors didn't surrender, not even in the face of death. They'd have to knock him out or break him before he slumped down in defeat.

An opening showed itself and Dryce moved for it before he consciously thought to do so. One slip of his arm and a wrench of his shoulder sent the man on top of him flying onto his back with a dull thud and a groan of pain. But then the broad side of a forearm caught him in the face, stunning him for a moment, but not enough to take him back down. They exchanged blows, punching and kicking and parrying, neither strong enough to take the advantage.

A sweep at his legs from his second opponent made him jump towards the first, and they both crashed down, this time with Dryce on top. An arm wrapped around his neck from behind before he could pound the first man into the ground, but before Dryce could reach for it and do anything, a bell sounded and the man behind him let him go.

"Not too bad for a celebrity," his brother, Raze, said from his position beneath him.

Toran clamped his hand on Dryce's shoulder before stepping back to let him up. "Good showing," he said.

The three of them backed up to the bench on the side of the small training room and grabbed towels and water. They were all covered in sweat and the room around them reeked of it. "You're too much in your element, rolling on the ground like that," Toran smirked as he took a deep drink.

Dryce shuddered. "Not when it's my brother under me!"

Even Raze laughed at that, the sound no longer rusty after so many months of having his emotions back. It still filled Dryce with happiness to have his brother returned to him. As a soulless warrior, little remained of the man he'd once been, and it had pained Dryce every time they encountered one another. He'd made a point to pull back, to keep his distance. At the time he'd told himself that it would be easier for Raze if he acted like that, but he'd long since realized that he'd done it to protect himself. He knew Raze didn't hold it against him, and at the time he hadn't been able to feel the rejection, but now Dryce was making up for lost time, stealing moments with his brother during and after training when Raze wasn't ensconced with his own mate.

"Is the coming battle weighing on you?" Raze asked quietly, the unexpected question enough to confuse Dryce.

He scrunched his face up in question. "No more than it weighs on any warrior. This is what we've all waited for." Finally they had a chance to get justice for their ancestors, to end the threat that Yormas of Wreet and his allies posed to

Earth and punish him for all the harms he'd done. Yes, a part of Dryce feared what could happen if things went wrong, but it was small and far outclassed by the battle hunger within him. He'd been made for this, had trained for it since he was old enough to hold a blaster. "Why do you ask?" They spoke quietly even though the training room was closed off from the rest of the gym. No one could overhear them, but still, speaking of doubts on the eve of battle was not something to be done in more than a whisper.

"Kayde said that you haven't gone out for the last week. He asked me if you'd said anything about that." The concern on Raze's face was almost enough to make Dryce laugh.

Was he really such a scoundrel that a week without taking a stranger to bed was enough to have his friends worried for his wellbeing? He supposed it was better than having them judge him for his promiscuity, but he hadn't realized that no one thought that he was capable of sleeping alone.

Truly, he had suffered his restlessness over a few of the last nights, but it seemed that his Peyton liked to stay up late as well. They'd exchanged silly messages until well past midnight and while sleep still hadn't come easy, he hadn't felt any need to venture out to find a companion.

"It has nothing to do with the ships on the horizon," Dryce promised. "A little more than a week ago I went out one night and I saw my denya."

The two men beside him froze. "Your denya?" Toran asked. "Why didn't you tell us?"

"Because when I said that I saw her, that's what I meant. We still haven't met, haven't bonded. I glimpsed her from across the room and… that was it." He wished that he had a better image of her in his mind. She was mostly a silhouette of dark hair and soft skin. He would have asked for her to send him a picture, but if she asked the same in return she'd know who he was and he might ruin everything.

"So what are you doing about it?" Toran pressed. "You saw her once and that's it? Have you made an effort to find her?"

"Things have been a bit busy lately, wouldn't you say?" Dryce pointed out. "And we've been sending messages to one another. She dropped her communicator that night and I found it."

"Then why don't you meet?" Raze asked. "You can't claim your denya over messages on a communicator."

"Really? I hadn't realized." Dryce shook his head. He didn't want to admit what she'd said about him, didn't want to hear if his brother and his friend agreed that he was charming and slick with no substance. Dryce pushed himself off the bench and stretched. He was about to offer the men another round on the mat to keep from answering more questions before the wall comm activated. "NaLosen, NaFeen, and NaFeen, report to the third floor immediately."

The three of them exchanged looks, but no one knew what it was about. They took enough time to change out of their sweaty uniforms into something more presentable and hustled up to the third floor where Sandon and General Alvarez were waiting along with Druath and Kayde and two other humans that Dryce didn't recognize and one he did.

Peyton.

Denya.

The recognition didn't tear through him so violently this time, but he felt a pull towards her and wanted to step closer, wanted to touch her and breathe in her scent, wanted to feel the heat of her body against his. She was so close to him, and yet she had no idea who she was.

No. As she took in him and his fellow companions, he remembered that she knew exactly who he was, and once she realized it she barely suppressed a scowl.

Dryce wanted to reach for his communicator and wave their messages in front of her as if to prove that he was more than she thought he was, but he feared that if he did that she would think that he'd been using her, had been holding their messages close in some sort of mockery, something he'd never do. So he took his seat beside his fellow warriors and did his best to ignore Peyton as if she meant nothing to him.

She was here for a reason, and only then did he wonder what she was doing on an SDA base. Did she work for the SDA? In all their communications, they'd shared only a few facts about themselves. He knew she had a sister and that her parents had passed away, but she hadn't spoken of her work or much more of her past. He knew she loved dogs and had a soft spot for twentieth century vehicles, that she'd built her first robot when she was twelve years old and used it to terrorize her sister. She watched scary movies by herself on the darkest night to make them more terrifying but refused to watch anything romantic. She loved coffee but tried not to drink it too often, and her favorite vegetable was cauliflower. He knew more about her than he'd known about any lover, and more than he knew about most of his friends. And yet she still didn't know his name.

Raze smacked him on the leg to bring his attention back to the room around them. Sandon was talking about a breakthrough that the human tech team had made, nodding at Peyton and the two humans beside her.

"The ships sitting at the edge of the solar system are enough to damage Earth, but as best we can tell, they can't hope to destroy the planet. In a full scale attack, they might be able to hit half a dozen cities before our defenses could subdue them. However, given Yormas of Wreet's long tenure as an ambassador on the planet and his vast connections, we've long thought that an attack from space was the secondary threat." Sandon pulled up a series of slides on the holo player which gave a brief history of Yormas of Wreet and explained their current intelligence.

The news that the Oscavians and Wreetans in the sky were a secondary threat was a surprise to Dryce. No one had whispered about a land-based conflict. The humans were more or less unified when it came to threats from outer space, and though Yormas had lived on the planet for many years, if he'd brewed conflict between human factions, none of it was simmering to the surface at the moment.

"Further analysis of the data recovered from Fenryr 1 has given us chemical signatures that Yormas's weapon left in the wake of the attack. We also see spikes of certain types of radiation just before it was deployed. Detya and Earth share similar environments, and in the past weeks we've seen similar radiation spikes. The SIA is convinced that Yormas has smuggled his weapon down to Earth. This has not been the opinion of the SDA or the Detyen Legion, but Dr. Cho has some information that seems to substantiate the SIA's claims."

He nodded to her and Peyton took a deep breath. She stared at a small tablet in front of her before finally looking up at the gathered group. She cleared her throat before speaking. "Hello. My name is Dr. Peyton Cho. My team works in the SDA science division studying and re-purposing recovered alien tech. Three days ago we were assigned to study and catalog a series of items from an Oscavian shuttle used by a hostile alien. My associate, Lilah," she nodded to a woman with long red hair and a pinched expression, "was the one to make the discovery."

Peyton tapped at her tablet and data streamed over the holo player. It was too disjointed for Dryce to read, but Lilah's eyes scanned over it as if she was making sure that everything was there. "The data was contained in what we think was some kind of ignition switch. There are three sets of coordinates," as she spoke three lines of numbers were highlighted, "and aerial surveillance has shown some anomalies, as if the signal was being obfuscated there. We believe that this ignition switch is one that could be used to set off something like what destroyed your planet." She paused and her eyes seemed to be drawn to Dryce. Their gazes locked for a moment before Peyton tore herself away. "And if that is so, then the device will be at one of the locations listed. They are all relatively remote, but accessible by land vehicles and near enough to cities that any aliens might not draw undue attention. We think that we've managed to create a kill switch using the tech we've recovered, so once the sites are investigated, the team can disable any weapon they find." She nodded towards Sandon and leaned back in her chair.

"We can't let the populace know about the weapon," said Sandon. "It would cause panic and could make us more vulnerable to attack. Dryce, as the lone unmated warrior on your team, will take point. He and his partner will infiltrate the locations and disable any device they can find. Raze, Toran, and Kayde will be your field support." Raze seemed ready to protest that Dryce had found his mate, but this time it was Dryce's punch against his thigh that kept him quiet.

General Alvarez cleared his throat.

Sandon took a deep breath and paused as if it pained him to say the next part. "Sierra Alvarez will temporarily be deputized as a member of the Detyen Legion and join you. Druath NaKam will run your op from headquarters."

Dru opened his mouth to protest, but Sandon spoke over him. "If you do this successfully, you will prevent a war and save billions of lives. We could not save our home, but we can make this our new one. Any questions?"

Determination blazed through Dryce. This was his chance to prove himself to Peyton and the Legion, and to save Earth from certain destruction. But he did wonder about one thing. "What partner?" If Raze, Toran, and Kayde were his support, who else was there?

He sensed Peyton stiffen and when Sandon's eyes fell on her, he realized why. "Dr. Cho."

***

"What?" Peyton didn't realize that she'd spoken aloud until all heads swung her way. The pretty boy, Dryce NaFeen, gave her a strange look, but she didn't see the rejection she would have expected from a trained soldier. Commander Sandon looked puzzled by her question, most likely because he'd explained much of the plan to her before bringing it to his people. She cleared her throat and did her best to ignore the burning of her cheeks. "Are you sure it's best to send in the two of us alone?" she managed to ask. "I wouldn't want to cause problems by not being military trained." That sounded okay, she was almost certain. She couldn't exactly tell the gathered group that Dryce made her feel funny and she didn't want to spend extra time around him.

"You will have support from NaFeen's team," Sandon assured her. "You won't be alone."

And still Dryce was staring at her like he knew her. What was that about? Peyton did her best to keep her gaze on anyone but him. She'd heard stories and she didn't want the guy to get any ideas, especially not when they were going to work together. She was sure that as soon as they were forced to speak to one another she'd be reminded why she was wary of him in the first place, but right now her best option was avoidance.

She paid attention as Sandon laid out the rest of the details and pulled up extensive maps that covered the areas they would infiltrate. She and Dryce would have use of a two-person aerial speeder to quickly get in and out of the compounds, while the Detyen team would be using ground vehicles and drones to cover them from a distance.

Peyton hadn't wanted to be assigned this job, but as soon as they found the maps and the trigger she'd been certain someone on her team would be assigned to the field. If they'd had more time, they might have been able to train one of the soldiers to disable the devices they expected to discover, but with the rush she was going to be using a huge mix of training and instinct to disable a device that might be capable of destroying the planet. Someone with only basic tech training didn't stand a chance. Peyton very much doubted that there would be a simple kill switch on any of the devices, and if what she and her team had engineered from their discovery didn't work, she'd need to do some quick and dirty engineering to save everyone's lives.

Fiona was a better candidate for time in the field. She'd endured a tour as an SDA soldier before going to school and coming back to work in the tech department. But what she had in martial prowess, she was still learning in applied engineering. Peyton was the most trusted on their team when it came to the tech, and though she doubted she would make much of a soldier she knew she had the grit to do one mission.

But when Sandon, her team, and General Alvarez left, leaving her alone with all of the Detyens, she wondered if she'd bit off more than she could chew.

It didn't matter. The fate of the world was on her shoulders and she would do what she had to do to make sure she didn't fuck it up.

She looked at her new team, trying to put names to faces. The one who looked most like Dryce was his brother Raze, she remembered. He had a sour look on his face, but it wasn't aimed at her. The golden one beside him was named Toran and he was the leader, according to Sandon. That meant the blue one was Kayde and the purple one who'd almost objected to the assignment earlier was Dru. Sierra Alvarez wasn't there, but as a human woman, she'd stand out easily enough.

"I thought you were the one they drag out for the interviews." She lobbed the observation at Dryce, only realizing how confrontational it was as the words came out. *That* was a wonderful way to start their mission. God, he was sure to hate her by the end of this meeting. And she was going to screw everything up.

But Dryce had a thoughtful look on his face that transformed into a deadly smile as he leaned in towards her. "I've always been more than a pretty boy."

Raze groaned and tilted his head back. If it hadn't been obvious by look alone that they were brothers, that long suffering groan would have given it away. She gave Raze a sympathetic look. "You're the older one, aren't you?"

He nodded.

"I'm sorry. Younger siblings, right?" Not that she would ever put Ella on the same level as Dryce. Ella could be annoying, but she had never seemed so… *slimy* before.

Though in person Dryce didn't seem nearly as bad. And that was part of his evil sexy powers. Or it was the fact that he'd barely spoken since entering. He radiated an effortless sensuality that both attracted and repelled Peyton. She wanted to get closer and see if touching him could really be as satisfying as promised. But she'd never been one to share, and judging by the stories that had wormed their way through the SDA, Dryce didn't do anything *but* share.

"I am sitting right here," Dryce shot in, and there was none of the smooth seduction she'd expected, only an affronted little brother which somehow transcended the hundreds of light years the Detyens had crossed to make it to Earth.

Maybe this wouldn't be so bad. Maybe Dryce's reputation was mostly false, and it certainly shouldn't matter if he went through lovers faster than most. If he was a worthy soldier—and given the way his team was treating him, she didn't doubt that—they could complete this mission.

And once it was done and no longer so strictly classified, she could message DF and tell him exactly what kind of person Dryce turned out to be. She hadn't managed to message her new friend since she and her team had been entrusted with the Oscavian rubble, but she promised herself that she'd make time before she had to leave. Even if she couldn't tell him why, she wanted to message him at least once more before the end of the world.

Chapter Five

Raze didn't have much of a temper. Years as a soulless warrior had blunted his emotions, and though they'd grown anew since he claimed his denya, he had more control than he'd ever had before his sacrifice. But he spent the rest of the meeting with Dr. Cho caught between anger and amusement. His brother was walking a fine line, trying to tease the human who was his denya without letting her know about their connection.

It was all bound to blow up in his face, but Raze had to let Dryce sort that mess out himself. He had his own problems.

Sierra joined them a little after Sandon left and his heart lifted as it always did to see her. But from the cautious expression she sent him, she confirmed what he'd suspected the moment Sandon announced she'd temporarily be joining their team. She'd lied to him. Repeatedly.

For hours there was nothing he could do about it and he retreated back into the cold mask he'd worn for three years as a soulless warrior. The decision was made, Sandon and General Alvarez convinced of Sierra's usefulness, and there was no hope of him dissuading them from using her. Raze wanted to clutch at her and demand to know what she was thinking, but with everyone in the room he could do nothing but seethe.

Night was crawling in by the time they broke with plans to meet again in the morning and begin an accelerated training regimen for Dr. Cho. They only had three days before the mission would begin, so they were more concerned about defining Cho's limits rather than teaching her anything new. This whole plan was running on momentum and prayers, and Raze only hoped it didn't fall apart before they found out if Yormas of Wreet had managed to smuggle his weapons onto the planet.

Sierra tried to slip out and away from him, but Raze caught up with her quickly and casually draped his arm around her shoulders. She melted into his side, walking seamlessly with him as they'd done since their mating several months before. And with every step his anger was blunted as another emotion opened up a yawning chasm in his chest.

"If you're going to yell, at least wait until we're in the car," Sierra muttered. She was fully aware of what she'd done, he could tell, and unrepentant.

"I'm not going to yell," Raze promised. "But that doesn't mean I have nothing to say."

She wrapped her arm around his back and they walked in step to the parking garage where her vehicle was waiting. It was deadly quiet as they drove home, though the packed streets filled with commuters racing home at the end of their days were a needed reminder of just why they were both working so hard and risking so much.

"You told me that you were happy working on coordination between the SIA and SDA when we talked about this." Raze had wanted to wait until they got home, but with traffic this dense that could be more than an hour, and he didn't want his anger and his hurt to build again.

"I didn't do this to hurt you." Sierra quickly glanced his way before darting her eyes back to the road. "Dad approached me. I would have told you if this was my idea."

"And you didn't think to tell me when it wasn't? I thought we discussed things together. I know you've been looking for something since the SIA fired you, but things have changed and you're risking more than just yourself when you go into battle." He didn't yell, as promised, but only just. His heart pounded madly in his chest and he wanted to pace, to move. Maybe starting this conversation in the car hadn't been the brightest idea.

"He came to me last night," Sierra gritted out. "I have not seen you since he asked. I would have mentioned it before Sandon sprang it on you, but this wasn't your decision to make. I'm a trained operative, you've seen me in the field. Don't discount my skills just because I'm suddenly your mate." Her fingers gripped the steering wheel so tightly that her skin had gone bone white.

"I would never discount your skills, I'm only alive and whole because of you. But running into danger now—"

"I'm not running into it, Raze, it's running towards us!" She took the nearest exit and pulled into an empty parking lot, throwing the car into park and turning towards him. "The world is going to end if we don't do something to stop it, and I can't let this hold me back from doing everything I can to help!" She placed her hand on her still flat stomach and looked at him, her eyes unfathomably deep and full of longing. "Our timing is kind of crap. I want there to be a world for our child to be born into, we can't just sit back and stay out of danger. And don't you dare chastise me for agreeing to be support for this mission when you didn't do a thing to hold back."

He reached out and placed his hand over hers, the hope of their new family blossoming in his heart. "I don't know what I would do if something happened to you." He leaned in and nuzzled against her cheek, pulling her scent in deep and letting it envelope him. This was his mate; she carried their child, the hope of a new Detyen race, and she was about to join him in what could easily descend into a deadly mission.

Sierra's hand came up and she ran her fingers through his hair. "Do you think I'm any different? I never realized what it was like to need someone before, but I can't go back now, not now that I've found you. You're *everything* to me, Raze, my beating heart."

"I can't stay back." He didn't think about all of the things that could happen when he put on his armor; if he spent his days fearing the worst, he'd have no time left to cherish his mate or plan for their future. "I'm a warrior."

"And so am I," Sierra insisted. "My own *father* came to me to ask that I join up. Do you think he wants me in danger?"

His fingers curled over her stomach. "He doesn't know."

She kissed his cheek. "None of them do yet, it's far too early to tell anyone." She kissed him again, her lips trailing down his chin and neck until she found one of his clan markings and traced it with the tip of her tongue, making Raze shiver and his cock throb to life.

"You're trying to seduce me into seeing things your way," he said, but it came out huskier than he intended.

Her hand trailed down until it rested on his thickening cock. "I know, is it working?" He could feel her grin against his skin and knew that he was hopeless to hold out against her.

But they weren't done talking, and he hadn't surrendered all of his faculties yet. "You can't just put yourself in more danger every time someone *asks*." The last word came out a gasp as she cupped her fingers around him and stroked him through his pants. He arched up into her touch and his hands gripped the sides of his chair to keep from reaching out to her. "You're devious."

Sierra tipped her face up towards him and grinned. "You're mine."

"Always, denya." He captured her mouth and devoured her, inhaling her now familiar taste, the taste of home.

When she pulled away they were both breathing hard and Raze was certain that his eyes had gone red. Sierra eyed him, her expression grave. "I'm not pulling out of the mission. But you have my word that I won't take any unnecessary risks. And I expect the same from you. We're going to meet this threat together, and we're going to deal with it. And once things settle down, we can tell everyone about the new life we're bringing into this world and watch the chaos as they try to deal with that. Got it?"

They could argue for the next three days, Raze knew it. And the outcome would be the same. His denya was determined to do her part, and she had the training and experience to know her limits. He feared for her and the child she carried, but the only thing he could possibly do that might keep her from the field was explain the situation to her father, and he would not do that to her. So Raze let the argument go and surrendered to her kiss.

And when Sierra engaged the privacy shields on the window, he surrendered to so much more.

Chapter Six

Peyton: They're going to kill me. I'm not built for this!

DF: What? You don't seem like a quitter.

Peyton: New project at work. I think I angered someone in a past life.

DF: Past life?

Peyton: Figure of speech. Not a thing where you're from?

DF: We have figures of speech.

Peyton: :) I meant past lives as a concept.

DF: Not among my people.

Peyton: I'm being called away. I'll try and message later, but this project may end up taking more than a week. So if I go silent, start praying for me.

DF: Best of luck!

Peyton looked down at the chat log and wondered if she should start up the conversation from a few hours ago again. She'd finally snuck away from the training that the Detyen team had inflicted on her, mostly from Kayde and Sierra. Dryce hadn't shown up yet, but they'd told her that he had other duties that morning and he'd be there in the afternoon to take over. They needed to learn to work together before they set out.

Wonderful.

She was pretty sure if she sent an SOS to DF he would come rescue her, but she wasn't cowardly enough to do so. Or brave enough. She still didn't know his name, and she hadn't asked him to send a picture. Neither of them had discussed meeting in several days and she was both pleased and disappointed by that. It was fun to have someone she could talk to without worrying that they'd judge her. But the more she talked to DF, the more she *wanted* to talk to him. He'd send her funny thoughts in the middle of the night or share stories of his homeland. She especially loved the anecdote he'd told her about his brother hiding all of his shoes in the snow on his first day of training which made him late and barefoot. He'd gotten his brother back by placing his warmest jackets in the deep freezer until they were solid.

The tricks had seemed mean to her, but to him they'd just been a part of life.

She stuffed her communicator back into her bag rather than send a message. She needed to keep away from DF until the mission was done. He sucked up too much of her focus and it was better to get used to not talking to him now than to be missing him a lot once they were out in the field.

And when she was back she'd ask him if they could meet. Her hand was still holding her communicator and she pulled it back out. If she waited until the mission was done, she was going to chicken out. But now that she was thinking about it, she could do it and be done. Peyton took a deep breath and pulled up the chat log again.

Peyton: This is for real my last message for a while. But when I get back, how about we get that drink?

The sound of a message notification almost made her jump, as if she was hearing DF receive the message. But when she turned around after turning her comm off and stashing it in her bag for good, she saw that it was only Dryce reading his own communicator, a wolfish smile on his face. He looked up and that grin grew even more predatory.

Peyton shivered and stood. She didn't want to be on her knees around that man. Who knew what ideas would climb into her mind and take over.

"What has you looking so happy?" Sierra asked, reminding Peyton that she and Dryce weren't the only people in the room. Funny how that happened. Once she set eyes on the captivating Detyen it was like everyone else melted away.

She needed to get a hold of herself.

Dryce tapped out a response and glanced up at her before shifting his gaze to Sierra. He looked... bashful. That couldn't be right. But he stuffed his own communicator into his bag and whatever she thought she'd seen was gone, replaced by the grin she already wanted to run from. "Just setting up a date," Dryce said.

Sierra and Kayde both looked at him with narrowed eyes, and for some reason Sierra glanced at Peyton for half a second, as if she had anything to do with this conversation.

"Raze said—"

He cut Sierra off. "We don't have much time to get our training done."

Sierra bristled and even Kayde didn't look pleased by that response. What did they expect? Dryce was clearly a dick who cared more about setting up a date with some random person than talking to his sister-in-law or the rest of the team. At least Peyton had turned *her* comm off after trying to set up her own date.

That she and Dryce were doing the same thing before a mission was not something she wanted to think about.

"We've covered some basic evasion techniques this morning," Kayde reported. "But we decided to wait until this afternoon to do any grappling. Sierra and I both have to report to Sandon, but Toran should be here shortly. Why don't you start working on something before then?"

Dryce nodded, all traces of his earlier grin gone. If she didn't know better, she'd think he was a serious soldier treating this mission with as much care as it needed to be treated. Maybe she could believe that if she wasn't sure that his mind was on whatever piece of ass he was meeting afterward. "We'll start on breaking out of holds," Dryce decided and they bid Kayde and Sierra farewell.

That left Dryce and Peyton alone for the first time, and though Kayde and Sierra had left, the small training room they were in suddenly felt all the smaller. They'd chosen the room so the warriors wouldn't gawk at her or wonder why a human was training with elite Detyen Warriors during such a critical time, but now Peyton wished they were out in the main room. She might not have liked Dryce, but her body hadn't gotten that message, and she feared that when he touched her she was going to burn up from the inside.

"Who's the date?" she forced herself to ask. She didn't for a second want to forget who Dryce truly was.

And if she'd expected him to take offense to that or shut her down, she was surprised by the happy grin that nearly split his face in two. "Someone special."

"I've heard that you only do special for the night." This kind of venom wasn't like her, but normally her brain was firmly in control. If she couldn't stop her body from wanting Dryce, she seemed determined to make sure he didn't want her. It was like she was possessed, and she didn't know how to stop. It might have been the stress of the mission weighing down on her, but a part of Peyton was horrified by how she was speaking. She prided herself on her control. And two minutes with Dryce and it all went out the window.

Metaphorically. The room they were in had no windows, only dour cinder block walls.

"You don't think a man can change?" he asked, sounding truly curious, as if her acerbic response had been nothing but pleasant.

Peyton forced herself to take a deep breath before she responded, and was glad that the not so nice smell of the gym and training room around them was strong enough to overpower whatever natural scent Dryce gave off. She would go crazy if he smelled as good as he looked. "Sure," she conceded. "People can change if the reason's good enough. But staying changed is usually harder than the big change in the first place."

Her father had been like that. Her mother had told them the story a hundred times about how he'd been a pilot who flew to the far flung reaches of the galaxy and he'd given it all up at the age of thirty to settle down with her and have children. Except once Ella was born he got itchy feet, and first those feet took him to another woman's bed, and then back into space. When news came of his ship's destruction, her mother had cried for days. In the end her father hadn't been able to stay true to one woman or planet. Why should she expect it of anyone else?

Dryce peered at her as if he could see all of those thoughts racing through her head. It was eerie and a little terrifying the way he seemed to be able to look through her. She wasn't someone who needed to be seen; she did her job perfectly well ensconced in the bowels of her SDA lab, so falling under the attention of the biggest flirt in the entire Detyen Legion was something she wasn't sure she knew how to handle.

"Some changes are worth maintaining," Dryce insisted. "And sometimes they happen because of growth. Maturity. Fa—" he cut himself off and Peyton wasn't sure what he'd meant to say.

"Does it matter what I think?" she asked. "We're here to do a job, not become best friends." If she drew that line now, maybe she'd find a way to maintain it. She wasn't going to become his friend, and she really shouldn't become his lover.

"You're the one who can save us all. Of course it matters what you think."

"Let's just get this training over with. I need to check in with my team before dinner and I don't want to keep them waiting." She'd left her people to further study the detonator and map they'd discovered in hopes that with the three days of training she was being forced to endure they would find more information for the mission. Every day she was supposed to check in and see where they were, see if she had any other ideas to offer them. And she knew that she was going to be so exhausted by the end of the day that she wouldn't be much help. But a promise was a promise.

Dryce seemed ready to say something; instead he just nodded. "What sort of hand to hand combat training have you had?"

That startled a laugh out of her. "I'm a doctor, not a warrior." They shared a friendly smile and Peyton's stomach flipped. God, Dryce was handsome, a handsome bordering on beautiful that made her afraid to get too close. How could someone built like him be real? And how could he be the one she'd been partnered with to save the world?

This was all one messed up dream that she couldn't make sense of, but finding a way to make unfamiliar pieces fit was Peyton's job, and she was going to do that here just as well as she did it back in her lab.

"So not much?" Dryce clarified.

"Sierra and Kayde were the first people to teach me anything beyond how to make a proper fist." She'd stared down some asshole college boys before and she was always willing to fight to protect her sister, but her skills had never needed to match her determination. Until now.

"I'm sure your sister is happy you couldn't do anything more than that," Dryce said as he settled into some kind of stretch.

"How did you know I have a sister?"

***

Fuck. He couldn't say that the conversation between them had been going well, but it had been going, and Dryce wanted to savor the minutes he had alone in Peyton's company before they'd be thrown into danger. And now he had to go and mess things up with a few careless words.

"I thought you said something about a sister?" He floundered, trying to recover the conversation. "Perhaps it was in your file."

"You've read my personnel file?" Peyton crossed her arms and her jaw was set; she looked to be about a minute away from punching him. At least she knew how to make a fist. He wouldn't want her to hurt her hand any more than his skull was likely to damage it.

"A short bio, so I had knowledge of your background. For the mission." That was all true, and if Dryce dug into his mind, he was sure there was a mention of a sibling. He had to be careful if he didn't want to give things up. He'd charmed her enough over their messages that she wanted to meet him in person. Now he just had to be agreeable enough on the mission so that when they met afterward she wouldn't immediately go running off.

It had seemed a lot more likely before they started to talk.

Peyton's ire subsided and she nodded. "Of course. They gave me information about your team as well. Shall we get to work?"

It was torture. Payback for every wrong he'd ever done, every lie he'd ever told and all the sweets he'd stolen when he was a little kid. As Kayde had suggested, Dryce taught Peyton how to get out of a few simple holds, and those holds meant they had to get up close and personal. He could smell the shampoo she used in her hair and the floral scent of her skin. It was so soft against his calloused hands that he wanted to stroke and see what response he could elicit, but he forced himself to remain completely professional.

She was his mate, but she didn't know that yet, and it wasn't yet the time to tell her.

They'd gone over a simple wrist hold so many times that a faint bruise was starting to bloom on Peyton's skin. It was to be expected, bruises happened in training all the time, especially when working on a specific move like they were. But seeing the faintly darkened skin turned Dryce's stomach and he quickly shifted them to something else. He would never lay his hands on his denya in anger, would never do her harm, but if he didn't teach her these things now, she would be going into a dangerous situation without the tools necessary to survive it. So Dryce tamped down on all of his sharp protective instincts and funneled them into teaching his mate what she would need to know.

About an hour into their training Toran showed up.

"Talk some sense into him," Peyton said, crossing her arms, a funny look on her face.

"What?" Dryce asked. They'd been working well together for an hour, so what kind of sense was she talking about?

Toran looked between them and seemed to be trying to hide a smirk when he noticed Dryce step closer to Peyton. Dryce hadn't even realized he was doing it, and when he tried to step back and give her space he couldn't. Toran was a good friend, and a mated man. But Dryce didn't like how closely he was standing to Peyton. Peyton was *his*, and while the urge to claim her roiled through him the thought of letting another man close to her drove the darkest savage instincts inside of him.

"My mother could get out of his holds and she's been dead for years." Peyton crossed her arms and spoke to Toran as if Dryce were not in the room.

That wasn't true, he'd held her hard enough to bruise. "I'm teaching you the technique," Dryce insisted. What was the point of holding her hard enough to hurt if she didn't understand what she was doing?

Peyton closed her eyes and took two deep breaths before turning towards him. "And I understand the technique," she said with precise calm. "If I don't do it for real, I'll never learn it."

"You're already bruised." He pointed to her wrist. He wanted to stroke that delicate skin and kiss it until it was better, but she was already angry at him and she didn't like him in the first place. He had never realized how torturous it could be to be around his denya.

Peyton shrugged. "Yeah, I bruise easily. No big deal. Come on." She flicked her fingers, motioning him towards her as if this were the beginning of the sparring match. One she could not win, and he refused to fight.

Dryce looked over at Toran as if the older man could save him, but Toran's eyes were lit with humor. He knew exactly the turmoil that was going on inside of Dryce, but for some reason he had no sympathy.

"If you don't want to do it, ask your friend." Peyton was insistent, begging to be hurt, and

Dryce didn't trust Toran to touch his mate. He didn't want anyone doing that besides himself.

"No!" Both Toran and Peyton stared at him expectantly and Dryce knew they wouldn't accept that simple denial. "We're going to be partners," he reasoned. "I'll do it."

"Fine," his Denya said piercingly, "then do it."

He hadn't meant to go easy on her, despite whatever she thought. Dryce understood that they were going into dangerous territory, that they could meet deadly foes at any moment, and while he would lay his life down to prevent his mate from coming to any harm, he knew he had to give her the tools necessary to be able to save herself. He didn't know how Raze did it. But Sierra had already been a warrior when they met. Peyton belonged in her lab, and in Dryce's bed, not anywhere where blaster fire could burn her skin and cut her down.

He got a hold around her shoulders and took barely a second to savor the contact between them. In other circumstances he could stand like this for hours, but his mate didn't like him and they had a job to do. He was sure to grab tighter than he had earlier and when Peyton worked to get out of his embrace, he clutched even harder, making her struggle for it. But with the stamp on his foot and a twisted his arm she got out of the hold and he gave her a big smile of congratulations.

Peyton still didn't look happy.

"Even I can see that you're holding back," Toran, the traitor, said. Dryce wanted to ask him how he would feel if Iris were the one in the situation, but that would tip off Peyton to the fact that something bigger was going on, and if she knew that who knew how she would react? He hated to lie to her, to withhold this truth, but the mission depended on it.

"See?" Peyton pursed her lips, her brown eyes challenging.

She wanted a challenge? "Again."

They got back into position, this time with Dryce holding on as hard as he dared. When Peyton stamped on his foot he didn't move, even as he winced at the pinch through his boots. She tried again, twice in a row, surprising him enough that he lost his grip for just a moment, and she used the advantage to escape his grasp again.

"Damn it," Peyton spat, her frustration palpable. "If you don't think I can do this, tell your commander, otherwise do the damn training. I'm not wasting my day so that you can coddle me."

"That's not what I'm doing." If he'd been holding back before, he hadn't the last time, and she'd performed the move as well as any recruit.

But Peyton wasn't satisfied. "No?" She turned to Toran. "NaLosen, come over here and show him how to do this."

Toran took a step forward and this time Dryce couldn't stop the low growl that came out of his throat. He couldn't completely prevent the enemy from touching her, but he'd be damned before he let his own man near her.

Peyton spun towards him. "What is your damn problem?"

"He's not your partner, I am." Her partner, her protector, her mate.

They set up this time, and Dryce didn't let his grip loosen, no matter how much Peyton struggled. She wrenched against him, but every time she shifted he moved with her, until the hold was one she hadn't practiced evading and she didn't have the technique to escape. But his mate was nothing if not resourceful. She kicked at him and tried to stomp each of his feet, she used what little leverage she had to scratch at his exposed arm, and with a poke at his armpit, she made enough of a hole to get out. But Dryce wasn't done. He reached for her again and she spun, her fist out, and landed a blow on his nose hard enough to make him bleed.

Peyton's hands flew to cover her mouth as she immediately stepped back. "I'm sorry!" Her eyes were unbelievably wide and she looked horrified.

Toran laughed, and it was only that sound that reminded Dryce that he and Peyton weren't alone. "This is going better than I'd hoped," Toran said. "I'll be back with some ice. Try not to kill each other while I'm gone."

Peyton's horror at making Dryce bleed melted away. "No promises," she called to Toran's rapidly retreating back.

Dryce took a seat on the bench and couldn't help but smile. He might have been bleeding, but it could have gone worse.

Chapter Seven

Peyton ate, slept, and breathed the mission for those three days. She didn't feel any better equipped to fight an enemy, but maybe she could get out of one or two holds. She and Dryce didn't talk about anything besides their coming assignment, and that was fine. If she wondered why she sometimes caught him looking at her with a weird look on his face, it wasn't any of her business. He was probably thinking of the date he'd told them all he planned, or maybe he'd already moved on to the next person.

Whatever it was, it didn't matter. Even if sometimes she wanted to ask him exactly what he planned to do when he got back. Wanted to ask him why he felt the need to chase after so many lovers.

Despite the stories, he hadn't done anything untoward since they'd been placed together. And as far as she could tell, he had moved onto the base and stayed away from all of the alien/human hookup spots in the city. So if he was as much of a lothario as the stories suggested, he could put it on hold to get his job done. That was good to know. Not that Peyton had any reason to care. He was a good soldier, that was all. And maybe she'd misjudged him a little. It didn't mean that they were going to be friends, but maybe she wouldn't trash talk him to random strangers anymore.

Not that DF was a stranger.

She had snuck away to check if he'd responded to her request to meet and he had. As soon as she was back, she was going to message him and set up a firm plan. She couldn't wait.

Which made the fantasies that had been sneaking up on her over the last few days a bit… problematic.

Peyton had never been one to fantasize about a man. She dreamed about being recognized as a top name in her field, and about how she could change the world. Occasionally she even dreamed about what it would have been like if her family hadn't been torn apart by her father's need to escape. But she never dreamed of the dark pleasures that an alien lover could bring to her.

Had never. Until now.

Dryce snuck up on her like that. She'd be thinking about what the mission would be like, imagining the two of them alone in some dense forest, camped out and forced to huddle for warmth against the encroaching cold. And then she'd think about hot lips on her neck and questing fingers, about shed clothes and arching bodies. She wondered what Dryce looked like naked, if a nude Detyen looked anything like a nude human, and when those fantasies happened while she slept she'd wake up aching and wanting, ready to call out to Dryce and have him show her exactly what she was missing.

She'd even had one crazy dream where she planned to meet DF and when she showed up Dryce was sitting in his place. The shock alone had been enough to send her rocketing to wakefulness and trying to rationalize why she'd think something so crazy. DF was a funny, kind guy who'd taken the time to make sure her communicator had been returned to her. Dryce was… well, he wasn't what she was looking for, that was for certain. Even if her initial impressions of him weren't exactly correct, it didn't somehow turn him into prince charming.

And even if she wanted to, she couldn't afford to develop a crush on the man now. They were about to head into a dangerous mission and she had to think about him as a partner, not someone she was imagining kissing.

Even if his lips looked so damn kissable.

"Don't be worried, we'll have your back." Sierra Alvarez was helping Peyton complete her packing. She and the rest of the Detyens would be taking off by land in the early morning while Peyton and Dryce would leave by air a little later. Sierra seemed determined to make Peyton feel welcome, and Peyton was glad for it. It was a bit intimidating to be surrounded by towering, sexy alien warriors at all hours, and that was probably the main reason for Peyton's crazy dreams.

"I'm not worried," Peyton replied. She surveyed the tightly packed bundles of clothes and hoped they would last long enough. She and Dryce weren't supposed to be out for more than a week, and she had two changes of clothes and an extra pair of socks. It was probably a luxury, she was sure regular soldiers normally went with far less, but she wasn't a soldier.

"Really?" Sierra clearly didn't believe her.

Peyton shrugged. "I could sit here and imagine all the horrible things that could happen to me if something goes wrong, or I could sit and imagine what will happen if we don't stop the people out in space. But none of that is going to solve anything. Dryce seems capable enough, and as soon as I'm near the devices I'll be able to disable them, if they're there. Worry will just make me screw up."

"How often are you repeating that to yourself?" Sierra handed her a tube of regen gel and Peyton stuffed it away.

"Oh, only every fifteen minutes or so."

They shared a grin. "My first mission off planet I was sure we were going to end up stranded on some hostile land and never manage to get back home. Right up until I was strapped in for takeoff I wanted to run back home and tell my dad it was a bad idea and I'd stay on Earth. And then we were off planet and it was too late. But the mission went well, and I never wanted to back out after that."

"Your dad didn't want you to go?" It was a trip to think of the famous General Remington Alvarez as a doting and concerned father, but to Sierra, that was who he was. The man had single-handedly saved Mumbai from alien invasion, but Sierra was more likely to offer stories of him failing at cooking or trying to scare her first boyfriend.

"He wanted me in defense, not intelligence. We've had words." She gave a wry laugh. "He's not happy about how the SIA fired me, but I think he's a little glad I'm working with the SDA now."

"The SIA *fired* you? You're General Alvarez's daughter! And amazing in your own right," Peyton was quick to add when she realized how that sounded.

Sierra rolled her eyes. "I disobeyed orders in a big way. I'm lucky I didn't end up in prison. But I got Raze out of the deal, and we saved a bunch of lives. I'd do it again in a heartbeat."

Until she'd met Sierra, Peyton hadn't known the role she'd played in the Detyen arrival on Earth. Though the Detyens had given several media interviews, mostly through Dryce, they hadn't spoken much of their human counterparts who had led them to the planet. But Sierra and her team of Sol Intelligence Agency operatives had met a team of Detyen warriors on a desolate scrap of dirt called Fenryr 1 where she and the Detyens had freed a dozen human women and discovered the ship that implicated Yormas of Wreet in the destruction of Detya. She'd also fallen in love with Raze while the whole thing was happening, and from the way all the Detyens looked at her, that was somehow more amazing to them than everything else.

"What's it like, being with one of them?" Peyton wasn't sure if she was thinking about DF or Dryce, but either way her mind was stuck on a Detyen man, and she didn't know what she had in store if something more than a flirtation came out of it.

Sierra got a far off look in her eye and grinned sweetly. "I feel like such a sap when I think about it. It's not common for a Detyen to find a human denya, and it was supposed to be impossible for Raze, but from the moment I met him, I just knew that there was something there I couldn't ignore."

"Denya?" Peyton thought she'd heard that word before, but she hadn't bothered to wonder what it meant. But now that Sierra brought it up, it seemed to mean that Raze was more than just her boyfriend.

"It means mate." Suddenly she became clinical, as if she were reading the definition out of a book. "Detyens recognize their mates on sight, and there is a strong pull between them. Often this leads to love, but sometimes they will just bond and leave one another to live their own lives."

"I didn't realize that Detyens were like that." Peyton had heard of fated mate bonds in news reports and media shows, but they'd always sounded a bit farfetched to her. But she wasn't about to say that to Sierra, not when the woman had risked her life and future for one of those Detyens.

"How's working with Dryce been?" Sierra thankfully changed the subject. Peyton didn't know why, but talking about fated mates made her feel strange, like there was something she was missing, some piece she didn't yet understand. It was like an itch covered by a bandage, something she wanted to pick at but knew that would make her bleed.

"Since it appears I'm talking to his sister-in-law… it's been fine." She was still mapping out all of the relationships on the team. Raze and Dryce were brothers, Sierra was Raze's mate, and the rest had worked together on various missions, and all of them were friends. Except her. She was one of two humans, one of two women, and floundering because she had no history with these people and no reason to build one. Once the mission was over they'd all go their separate ways.

If they survived.

Sierra nudged her shoulder and offered a smile. "If you want to complain, I promise, I'm a vault."

Peyton didn't want to complain, not exactly. She wanted to ask Sierra if she was crazy for the thoughts she was having about Dryce. Wanted to know just how guaranteed she was to get hurt if she let her guard down and tried to see where things could go between them. But despite Sierra's promise, Peyton didn't delude herself. If she revealed to Sierra that she had a... crush on Dryce, that would get back to everyone and the man would be insufferable.

On the bright side, his insufferability would probably obliterate any fond feelings she had in no time. But she didn't want to deal with the humiliation that would come before that.

"We'll get the job done well enough," Peyton said. "So let's get finished packing so we can get started."

***

Dryce sat in the pilot's seat with Peyton by his side, the engines humming as they prepared to embark on their mission. An eerie sense of calm settled over him. An entire lifetime had led to this moment, and if they were lucky, in a matter of days it would all be over. The threat to Earth would be taken care of, the destruction of his people would be avenged, and he would reveal himself to his denya and hope that she could accept him for the warrior he was and not the slick playboy he'd once been.

Peyton gripped the edge of her seat and took deep breaths, trying to steady herself. Dryce wanted to reach over and offer her words of encouragement, but each person had their own rituals before a mission and he couldn't interrupt hers just because she looked to be about thirty seconds from panic. Slowly her fingers loosened and she opened her eyes, staring out of the giant window in front of them. The speeder they'd been given was more like an early human aerial device called a helicopter rather than the sleek spacecraft he was used to. They wouldn't be able to break atmo, but what they gave up in power they gained in stealth.

The thrust came from a bladeless rotor which circled overhead and was much less susceptible to weather conditions than its primitive ancestors. He and Peyton were essentially sitting in a giant bubble and once they lifted off they'd be able to see far into the distance and it would be almost like they were floating. Dryce had spent plenty of time in a simulator learning to fly the human craft and he knew that Peyton had been given emergency lessons, but she didn't seem as excited to finally be taking off.

"We'll be perfectly safe," Dryce assured her. "We shouldn't encounter any hostiles, and even if we do, the stealth settings on this craft are some of the best available."

Peyton let out a shaky breath. "Not worried about that." She stared out the window in front of them but it didn't look like she was seeing anything but whatever was going on in her mind.

"Then what? Are you unwell?" The mission couldn't be delayed, but he would do whatever he could, short of stopping everything, to see to his mate's comfort.

"Not a big fan of heights," Peyton bit out. "I'll get over it."

"You're scared of *heights*?" Dryce didn't mean for it to come out so surprised, but he found it hard to believe that Peyton was scared of *anything*. She projected enough strength and confidence to cow a general and even knowing the secrets she'd shared with him in their messages he never would have guessed that something so banal could set her on edge.

"Yes," came her tortured confirmation. "It's quite common, I'll get over it. Let's just do this."

"No." Dryce leaned back in his seat and took his hands off the controls, looking towards his denya.

"No? You're going to put the planet at risk just because I'm a little nervous?" She sounded incredulous, and she turned to him, eyes narrowed, and no longer paying attention to the windows in front of them.

"The planet can wait a minute, you can't." Dryce offered her his best grin and almost laughed when she scrunched her eyebrows down, clearly perplexed by his reaction.

"I'll be fine," Peyton insisted. "I can do this."

"There's nothing you can't do," Dryce agreed.

"Don't patronize me," she snapped.

His smile wanted to falter, but he kept it plastered in place. Could his mate not see that he just wanted to ease her through this difficult situation? "I'm not, I promise."

Her expression evened out, even if it remained a bit suspicious. "Okay."

"Now I'm going to signal Dru and once he gives the go ahead I'm going to lift off. Keep your eyes on me until I tell you otherwise." He had no idea if this would make things better or worse, but he had to do *something* for Peyton.

"Oh, so this is just an excuse to get me to stare at your pretty face." Her eyes widened and she snapped her mouth shut as she finished the thought, a faint blush coloring her cheeks.

Dryce didn't shout in triumph, but it was a close thing. He'd known she thought he was attractive, even if she discounted all of his other qualities, but he'd never expected to hear her say it. "You think I'm pretty?" He gave an exaggerated simper and wanted to celebrate again when it forced a laugh out of her.

She didn't want to like him, he knew that. But he was making progress. If the mission went well, maybe by the end she might think of him as more than a useless pretty boy, might see him as the mate he could be.

If she didn't feel betrayed when she discovered he was the man she'd been messaging for weeks.

Doubt begin to creep in at the edges of Dryce's mind. He hadn't started their communication with any intention to deceive Peyton, and he hadn't explicitly lied to her. But the more they interacted in person, the more it felt like he was balancing on the line between truth and falsehood and one misstep would see him tumble over into the unforgivable.

He pushed those thoughts aside. They had a mission to carry out, and he needed to get Peyton through this despite her fears. Once they were on their way, he wouldn't have time to worry about the mixed up situation he'd gotten them into; his mind would be wholly dedicated to the mission and keeping his mate safe.

"You know you're too pretty for your own good," Peyton answered with a defiant smirk. "And I'm sure you use it to your advantage."

"It's all for you," Dryce said, more honest than he'd ever been in his life. "So keep your eyes here," he pointed towards himself, "and let's see where we can go."

Chapter Eight

Dryce wasn't supposed to be able to calm her down. No, if anything, Peyton's anxiety should have been skyrocketing as their helicopter lifted them into the sky and silently zoomed out over the city. But she kept her eyes glued to Dryce while they took off, watching the minute changes to his expression as they shifted from one gear to the next, going through the takeoff sequence like they'd done it a hundred times before.

Peyton's heartbeat threatened to kick into overdrive when she darted a glance out through the window beyond her partner's head, but some sixth sense he had made him reach out and grab her hand, pulling her attention back to him. His skin was unexpectedly warm, and though it wasn't the first time they'd touched, it *was* the first time he'd done it without the excuse of a training session.

"You're doing great," Dryce assured her, giving her hand a squeeze.

She squeezed back before pulling away. "How much longer?" she asked, proud that her voice didn't tremble. She was flying in a helicopter, the sky stretching beyond them on all sides and only the power of technology keeping them airborne.

That should have comforted Peyton. She could take the helicopter apart and put it back together without a manual and was confident that it would still fly. She knew exactly how a craft like this was meant to work. It was perfectly safe… as long as nothing went wrong. But flight had never been something she could reconcile her scientist's mind to. She wasn't going to climb into a space ship and trust the tech to ferry her through the vacuum of space, no matter how safe it was supposed to be, and trusting a helicopter now when she'd never even trusted a vehicle's anti-grav was as far as she was willing to go.

Ever.

"A few hours," Dryce replied. "We'll be landing about four kilometers away from our target. Cloaking will keep our ride out of sight if there are any hostiles at the location, but we should be able to pick up on them long before we land."

Peyton took several controlled breaths. Hostiles. Cloaking. This wasn't her life. "I belong in a lab," she finally sighed. "I'm not some soldier. I know why I was chosen, but this is so beyond anything I've ever done that I'm not sure I'm going to make it."

Dryce was silent for a minute, just long enough that Peyton began to wonder if she should have said what she did. He couldn't like that he'd been forced to bring a civilian with him. Maybe she should have been trying to prove to him that she was more than capable. But that wasn't her, and if she was going to have a panic attack the moment they landed, it was probably better that he knew it was coming.

"I will keep you safe," Dryce promised. "But your brain is the most important tool we have on this mission. I know you can do this." He said it with such sincerity that it blasted through all of the doubt she had when it came to him. His eyes met her, those unfathomably dark depths holding a promise of *something* that she was too afraid to look closely at. Who was this guy? Why was he like two different people? There was the playboy that everyone knew, and then also this competent soldier who looked at her like she held the world in her hand.

Both of them were too sexy for her own good, but Peyton wasn't going to tell that part to anyone. She could keep a hold of herself. Even if Dryce had just been the competent soldier and she wasn't guaranteed to get her heart broken by the playboy, she wasn't going to possibly fuck up their mission by letting *feelings* get involved.

Even though she wasn't going to let anything happen between them, Dryce's confidence buoyed her. She'd been chosen for this mission because she was one of the few people in the SDA who they trusted to get close to an unfamiliar piece of tech that could destroy the planet and disarm it.

"I can do this," Peyton echoed. Her heart flipped when Dryce's lips tipped up into a smile, but she wasn't about to get attached. No, she had to be strong, had to be mature.

Besides, she had a date with DF waiting for her when this was all done.

Peyton darted a glance at Dryce and then looked away, her emotions swirling in confusion. Sure, she didn't owe anything to DF. They hadn't made any promises. Hell, she didn't even know the man's name. But it wasn't like her to make plans with one man and start to develop feelings for another. *Not* that she was developing feelings for Dryce. That would be bad. Untenable. Certain to lead to heartbreak. She wasn't dumb enough to do something like that.

But when he caught her attention and pointed to a hawk flying in the distance, his face full of wonder at all of the life flourishing on Earth, her heart clenched and she wondered just how long she'd be able to tell herself that what she felt for Dryce didn't constitute *feelings*.

"So we're landing four kilometers away," Peyton prompted, trying to get everything back on track. They had a mission, and that was what they had to be dedicated to. "I assume we're covering the rest of the distance on foot?"

"Yes," Dryce confirmed. "If our scans and our back up show that it's safe enough to proceed, we go in on foot. We will do all of the recon we can, but we need to be on our way by nightfall. And we've been given strict orders not to engage with any hostiles."

"How am I supposed to disarm this bomb if we can't engage?" Peyton didn't need to be a soldier to know that didn't make any sense.

"We'll come back with a bigger team. We don't want to push them into using their weapon because one of the sites gets compromised."

And that meant that the mission was going to take even longer. Peyton leaned back in her seat, and not even the fact that she no longer seemed to be as nervous of flying could make her feel better.

***

When Peyton lapsed into silence, Dryce didn't try to push. Something was bothering her, but whatever it was would have to wait until later. He'd fix it if he could, but first they had to deal with their recon mission. Scans of the area didn't show any unexpected activity, but the enemy could easily be cloaked.

Based on what they'd learned from Brakley Varrow, they knew that the Oscavians and Wreetans had access to short range teleporters. If they'd set up reception stations in the forest, they could have easily sneaked in the parts for their weapon without triggering any of the defenses that were meant to intercept ships breaking atmo.

How long had they been preparing? If Yormas of Wreet had set himself on this path when he began his ambassadorship to Earth, the entire planet could be seeded with destructive devices and they would have no way of knowing.

Dryce would need to trust that the SDA, SIA, and the Detyen Legion were doing everything they could to make sure that wasn't true. They couldn't fight an enemy they couldn't see, but they could do their damnedest to destroy the weapons they discovered.

He set the helicopter down and engaged the passive cloaking tech that would ensure the vehicle remained undetected. Their packs were already prepared, so when he and Peyton hopped out of the helicopter, they strapped up and were on their way. Peyton followed a few paces behind him and the only sounds beside birds and bugs were their footsteps. Dryce was not used to operating in a forested environment, as most of his missions had taken place on space stations or densely populated cities, and his survival training had been done at Detyen HQ where it was winter all year round. The forest around them teemed with life, but with the trees so dense around them, he felt like someone could be watching them from any angle and they'd never know it.

But that was just his imagination. Or possibly their support team. He and Peyton would not be contacting his fellow warriors unless things went irrevocably bad, but they had to be near.

"Is something wrong?" Peyton asked, her voice cutting through the doubt and banishing his thoughts of being observed.

"No," Dryce responded. "Everything is fine." It was, he told himself. A warrior's instincts were his most important weapon, but that weapon could misfire when placed in an unfamiliar environment. None of his recon tools suggested they were being watched and there was nothing other than the feeling at the back of his neck that said otherwise.

Peyton made a noise, but said nothing else. Four kilometers wasn't a long walk, and though the forest was dense, they had no difficulty making a path. When they got close enough to see their target with their naked eyes, Dryce halted and Peyton followed suit.

He took a set of binoculars out of his pack and took a look around. Drone footage had shown an old house that was more memory than structure, a few beams holding up an old roof and only one wall still intact. Heat maps hadn't shown anything special about the location, but the coordinates had appeared on Brakley Varrow's trigger and they couldn't ignore it, even if the place looked like it had been abandoned more than a century ago.

The grass came up to their knees, but the trees gave way, only young growth making up most of the clearing around the house.

"As far as love nests go, it leaves a bit to be desired," Peyton said, coming to stand next to him. "Honestly, I'd expect better from you."

Dryce smiled, even if he wished that his denya wouldn't bring up his past exploits so often. He hadn't *once* mentioned anyone who'd come before her. He hadn't even meant to mention their upcoming date, even if she didn't know she'd invited him, but he'd been too ecstatic to hide his reaction when he received the message. But Dryce had a part to play here, and if this was how his mate wanted to joke, he'd play along. "I do try to provide at least two walls," he said. "It's no good if the roof comes crashing down in the middle of the main event."

Peyton laughed, the sound an intimate caress, one he was determined to hear more of from her, no matter what he had to do to elicit it. But that was later.

"Stay close," he cautioned. He had his blaster at the ready, but he doubted there were any hostiles to be found at this decrepit spot.

"Do you think this is a decoy?" Peyton asked, her voice cautiously quiet as they crept around. "Or were they here and gone?"

"I'm not sure. But we'll find out." A snap of the branches behind them had him swinging around, but it was only the wind that had him on edge. They continued on, carefully making their way closer to the old house, watchful for any traps or dangers on the floor.

They found nothing except an old patch of road that was so cracked it looked like no vehicle could pass over it on wheels.

"If anyone was here recently, they were using anti-grav," Peyton observed. "I don't see any tracks, and that mud over there," she pointed to a brown patch near a trickle of a stream, "would definitely hold tracks."

Dryce had to agree. "Let's check the house. There might be a basement, something hidden underground."

"I guess this isn't a *terrible* location for a secret underground lair," Peyton conceded. "You'd never guess from aerial shots."

"You could be right." If the basement was protected well enough, few of their scans would be able to pick up anything, and any readings they got might have been anomalies. Dryce didn't like it. "Keep behind me," he warned. They were both wearing armor, but that would only help so far.

The inside of the structure didn't look like anything more than a ruin. Dryce's foot almost went through a rotted floorboard in one place and Peyton tripped over some debris and would have fallen to her knees if she hadn't been standing close enough to Dryce to use him to brake her fall.

"Sorry," she whispered.

It was quieter in the house, the configuration of the remaining walls somehow blocking out all of the sounds from the forest around them. Eerie. That was the word for it. And that prickling at the back of his neck was there again, warning Dryce that they were being watched.

"Something is off here," he finally admitted. "I don't like it."

"Off? Off how?" Peyton didn't sound pleased by that, but she wasn't panicking, which was all he could ask for. She had no experience with problems in the field, no experience with the field at all. Despite her fear of heights earlier, she was doing better than some green warriors he'd trained.

"I'm worried we're being watched," he said.

Peyton spun around to the nearest opening and peered out into the forest, right in the same direction that Dryce would have guessed their observer was coming from. If anything could convince him that the threat was real, it was that. "I don't see anything. Do you think it's… who we're looking for?"

"No." The Oscavians and Wreetans would be shooting by now if they were out there. If they caught Dryce and Peyton, they had no reason to leave them alive. But he wasn't going to say that just yet. "It might be an animal, or someone who lives in these woods. We'll be cautious, but there's nothing else we can do just yet."

Peyton looked back at him for a long minute before she nodded. "You're the boss."

"Only until we find what we're looking for."

The structure was bigger on the inside than it appeared from the clearing around it, but it was clear that nothing but wind and wild animals had crossed the threshold in a long time. Even if it had been disguised to look abandoned there would have been signs of use. The dust and dirt wouldn't have been nearly as heavy, and the evidence of animal nests would have been easier to spot. As it was, Peyton shrieked when a pile of leaves started to move and a fat rat darted out of it.

"Have we seen enough yet?" she asked, voice too high to pass for calm.

Dryce wanted to say yes. They'd spent over an hour looking for anything, but they weren't quite done yet. "Soon," he promised, and hoped he wasn't lying.

"Fate of the world, fate of the world…" She whispered the mantra to herself as if it could ward off further vermin. Dryce kept himself from grinning too broadly. His mate was doing well and he didn't want to discourage her.

He found a latch that led to the cellar under a small pile of debris that might have once been an internal wall. It took both him and Peyton to heave the door open, the wood too warped by water and time to pull away smoothly. In the end he had to kick it several times until the cracks gave way and he and Peyton were able to pull the door up in rotten strips of wood.

Musty decay floated up from the dank hole where the house's cellar used to be and when Dryce pulled out his torch and lit up the darkness it was only to see mud, rotten wood, and a puddle that hid things that neither of them wanted to see.

"No one is hiding a secret lair down there," Peyton said with an air of finality. "But feel free to check. I'll just wait up here."

<u>Chapter Nine</u>

Dryce was in agreement and the two of them backed away from the dank entrance to the cellar and gave one final look at the ruin before leaving it behind to return to the helicopter. It was only then that Peyton remembered they'd have to get *back* in the sky to continue on their mission and she wanted to curse. Stupid helicopter. What was so good about air travel anyway?

"Any idea why they had this location marked?" she asked to try and distract herself. For some reason she'd expected Dryce to be chatty while they walked, but he'd been completely focused and nearly silent since they'd landed except for small bouts of conversation that she'd prompted.

"Didn't you suggest earlier that it could be a mistake?" Dryce shrugged. They had to move carefully down the path they'd taken to get to the house. It was barren enough to walk through the woods, but dense enough that branches brushed against them and they crushed the fallen twigs under their feet. "It might have been a place they scouted and discarded," he suggested.

"So you don't think we were lured out here on the off chance we intercepted that information, right?" She knew that there were hostiles *somewhere* on the ground, but she didn't want to think that they were waiting somewhere out there, obscured by leaves and branches, the sound of their movements hidden by the wind and animals who called this forest home.

"Probably not. Waste of resources." Dryce pushed aside a particularly large branch and waited for Peyton to pass before letting it go.

"Then what do you think was watching us? Or are we just being paranoid?" She hoped it was paranoia. The woods were dense and had to be full of animals. The Preservation and Animal Reintroduction laws of the last century had ensured that all kinds of animal populations were nurtured in areas where they'd before gone extinct. Including mountain lions, bears, and wolves. *Not* what she wanted to think about when she could just imagine all of those clawed beasts waiting to attack.

Dryce surveyed the land around them as if the trees could offer an answer. But finally he shrugged. "We remain on alert, but hopefully we make it to the helicopter without incident."

They walked. Peyton's calves cramped as they made their way up the incline to the plateau where they'd landed. It hadn't been so obvious on the way to the house that they'd been going downhill, but she could feel it now. She wanted to call for a rest when her leg seized up, but kept trudging on. Four kilometers was nothing to Dryce, who hadn't even broken a sweat. She wasn't going to be the weakling that held them back.

She was so focused on the pain in her leg that she ran into Dryce, who'd frozen in front of her. "What—" she began to ask before a growl from somewhere beyond the trees reverberated through her bones. Her tongue darted out to lick her suddenly dry lips and she looked around carefully as her body recognized an ancient predator even if her mind had yet to catch up.

"Keep moving," Dryce whispered to her, his body so tense she feared it would snap. "Slowly, but purposefully. Do. Not. Run."

She knew that. Everyone knew that. But as they took careful steps, her heartbeat kicked into overdrive and she wanted to break formation and sprint up the hill to the safety of the helicopter. All her fears of flying evaporated in the face of the threat on the ground.

A shaft of sunlight pierced the canopy of the forest and caught on a bit of gray fur. Wolves. A whole pack of them, if the rumbling growls growing closer and closer were anything to go by.

"Aren't they supposed to be afraid of us?" She grasped desperately for those lessons she'd learned about animals as a child, but she'd always been far more interested in mechanics and paid as little attention to life sciences as she could.

"It's your planet," Dryce shot back. "Shouldn't you be the one telling me?"

Now was not the time to argue, not with wolves surrounding them and ready to attack at any moment. "Shoot your blaster towards one of them," Peyton suggested. "That could scare them off." Loud noises, bright sounds, no animas were going to like that.

"Or they might attack. I would have shot them already if I thought I could get them before they got us." Dryce didn't sound panicked, which helped a little. Only a little. A pack of wolves were nearly close enough to touch and they didn't have much hope of making it to their vehicle before an attack.

"Do you have another suggestion?" she asked tightly. She and Dryce were barely moving now and one of the wolves had stepped out of the cover of the trees, ready to pounce as soon as they started running.

Dryce placed his hand on her arm. "If this doesn't work, I'll hold them off. You need to make it to the helicopter."

Hold them off? One man against a pack of wolves? Peyton was excellent at math, and she knew how that equation balanced out. "We go together," she insisted. "I'm not leaving you to die."

His fingers tightened. "You *need* to make it. The mission can continue without me. We start from the beginning without you, and we're running out of time."

She stared at Dryce as if she was seeing him for the first time. Gone was any hint of the playful playboy who seemed to be made of nothing but slick lines and nonsense. Here she stood next to a warrior and she prayed she didn't have to leave him behind. The man beside her just might be worth knowing, if she ever had the opportunity.

Dryce pulled away from her and levelled his blaster at one of the trees. He shot for a branch and for a moment nothing happened. Then a flash of red burst out and the branch snapped, crashing to the ground near one of the wolves. It yelped and bounded off and in quick order the rest of the pack followed.

And suddenly the woods around them were just forest again, no longer filled with dangerous animals ready to attack at the first instance of weakness.

Peyton wanted to sag to the ground in relief as exhaustion washed over her, but they kept trudging forward. And less than half an hour later they made it to their helicopter which was sitting where they'd left it as if nothing had happened.

Peyton kept glancing over at Dryce as they disengaged the passive cloaking and did a final investigation to make sure that nothing had tampered with their ride. He must have been satisfied, since he waved her forward to stash her bag in its proper compartment, his face as serious as it had been while staring down the wolves.

He'd been willing to die for her.

It was enough to make her stumble in her tracks. No one had ever sacrificed for her before, not even her parents. But this warrior who she'd insulted, who she'd thought was nothing more than a pretty face and an empty smile, had been willing to lay down his life to make sure that she could continue their mission. To make sure she remained safe.

If she brought it up, she knew that he'd say he would have done it for anyone, and that made her respect him even more. It showed her that he truly was the warrior he claimed to be, a piece of a greater whole that was going to save this planet.

The crush she'd been doing her best to ignore unfurled within her, emotions expanding until she feared that she couldn't keep what she was feeling off her face. She didn't know if she wanted to. They were in the middle of the forest, far away from home, and in the middle of a mission where they couldn't afford to get distracted.

But the intensity on Dryce's face when he caught her gaze did her in. She took two steps and closed the distance between them, tilting her chin up until she met his eyes. His startlingly *red* eyes. His nostrils flared and then they moved.

Her arms went around him as his hands cradled her hips and their lips crashed together in a kiss strong enough to topple every single restraint she'd been trying to put in place. His tongue darted against her lips and Peyton opened for him, longing for the taste she'd been dreaming about for longer than she'd cared to admit.

She was in trouble, and there was no place she'd rather be.

***

It was a battle to keep from touching her lips as they got back in the helicopter and flew away. Peyton had to keep her eyes trained ahead of her, otherwise she was going to stare at Dryce with far too much feeling. Was she fucking crazy? She was in the middle of a massive message flirtation with another guy and just went ahead and kissed the biggest player in the Detyen Legion.

And he'd kissed her back like the world was ending.

She could still feel the imprint of his hands on her and she wanted more. Wanted it now. Wanted *him*. That wasn't going to work. It couldn't.

But when she tried to open her mouth to explain the kiss away, to tell him that it was a mistake and it wouldn't be happening again, nothing came out.

In her head she could list the reasons it was a one off: they'd just survived almost being attacked by wolves, Dryce was the only other person there, he was too hot to be legal. And they weren't going to be attacked by wolves again, so the other two things didn't matter.

Her hands gripped the edge of her seat as Dryce engaged the engines and they lifted off. The one good thing about her raging panic was that it was too strong to be overwhelmed by her fear of flight. For the first time in her life, she almost *enjoyed* the view as they climbed higher and higher and she saw the forest stretch out like a sea of green all around them.

Yeah, she could understand why some people would love this. But she could also imagine what would happen if the engine failed and they plummeted all of those meters to the hard ground below.

Oh. There was the terror she'd thought that she'd avoided.

"Breathe," Dryce cautioned, taking his own deep breaths as if to show her how it was done. It was the first thing he'd said to her since they'd pulled apart and she didn't know if she was grateful for his silence or resentful.

Had the kiss been so commonplace that he didn't think they needed to say anything about it? Or was his mind just as mixed up as hers was? She wanted to ask. She didn't want to know.

Peyton sucked in a breath so deep it made her lungs hurt.

"And let it out," Dryce reminded her.

She didn't want to, but her body protested and her eyes watered, and she slowly deflated as her lungs emptied. "I don't like flying," she reminded him, as if she could make him believe that was the only reason she was having a problem right now.

"I'll make this as quick and safe as possible," Dryce promised.

It shouldn't have done anything to calm her. Why should she trust him when he said that? But he'd included safety, not just said that he was an experienced pilot. No, he would be as safe as he could while taking them to their next destination.

"I know." It came out as barely more than a whisper, but the promise settled Peyton's nerves as they flew onto the spot that had been designated as a safe place to camp for the night, out of the range of any of the coordinates that they were exploring.

The sun was starting to set as Dryce set them down and Peyton's stomach rumbled, reminding her just how long it had been since she'd last eaten.

"Our meal packs aren't exactly gourmet, but they'll settle your hunger," Dryce promised as he powered down the helicopter and pressed several controls that must have done something important.

"They can't be as bad as the shit I ate in grad school," Peyton muttered loud enough for Dryce to laugh.

"Don't be so sure," he said. "I'm almost certain these were devised by the soul—" he cleared his throat and looked away, his brow furrowed as he examined one of the controls.

"Is something wrong?" she asked. As far as flights went, the one they'd just endured was… not terrible. Peyton didn't want to contemplate their ride suddenly breaking down. She could fix it, of course, but her confidence in her mechanical abilities would definitely be put to the test. Ask her to disarm a bomb possibly capable of blowing up the planet? No problem. But fixing a helicopter she'd later need to fly in? No, thank you.

Dryce shook his head a little, as if he was trying to clear his thoughts. "No, no problems. We should get our tent set up before it gets dark. The warming block we've got stowed will heat up the food, which makes it slightly more palatable. And there's plenty of water."

That all sounded okay, until her brain wrapped itself around one point. "Wait. *Tent*? Singular?" She was supposed to lay beside Dryce all night in an enclosed space, surrounded by his body and his all too seductive scent? And somehow remain sane? Maybe it would be smarter to brave the elements.

"Yes." He seemed puzzled by her question. "Why would we need more than one for two people?"

"Because—" She bit her lip to keep from saying any more. Anything that came out of her mouth would be telling him far too much, and she didn't want his head to get any bigger.

But Dryce's expression shuttered and he didn't exactly frown, but he seemed hurt. "I would never do anything to you without your consent. If that is what you're worried about, I can sleep outside."

"I never said you would! I don't think that!" She wanted to reach across and grab onto him, to assure him that she didn't think he was the kind of guy who didn't take no for an answer. But she couldn't quite bring herself to admit that *saying no* was the problem. Because if he asked, she wasn't sure she had the strength to deny him.

Not after that kiss. Not after he'd said he would give his life for hers.

Dryce looked at her for several beats, still clearly pained, but he said nothing. Eventually he opened the door and unbuckled his restraints. "I'll begin to set up." And before she could respond, he left her there alone, more confused than ever.

Chapter Ten

Dryce had to get his temper under control. Discovering that he *had* a temper was a wonder unto itself. He'd never been one to lose control of his emotions, to let other's words anger him. But at the suggestion that he might do something harmful to his mate he wanted to protest and find a way to *make* her understand that she was with him, that no harm would ever come to her.

Of course, he quickly realized that forcing her to do anything was no good way prove that he meant her no harm. But the idea that he would force himself on her? That he would ignore her and take her without consent like some ravening beast or monster? If she thought him capable of that, perhaps there really was no hope for them.

He'd been so hopeful earlier, in those moments after her kiss. He'd never expected her to make a move, especially not so early in the mission, but if he closed his eyes he could still taste her against his skin, could still feel the press of her lips against his. He'd kissed and been kissed more times than he could count, but those few seconds with Peyton gave him more pleasure, more enjoyment, than the most sensual nights he'd ever had before. He could barely remember why he'd wanted others so badly when he sat next to her, those attractions mere embers to the blazing inferno that was his feelings for her.

He took a moment before reaching for their supplies, counting slowly and breathing carefully. By the time he was unfolding the tent he could think a little more clearly, and when Peyton joined him a few minutes later, it only hurt a little to think of what she'd suggested. Even if she'd immediately denied that was what she meant, he wasn't sure he could believe that. He knew what she thought of him. Why would she assume anything else?

They worked in silence and it only took a few minutes to anchor the tent and get their sleeping rolls set up inside. Outside Peyton set up the warming block and pulled out two meals, leaving them to heat on the softly glowing brick. It would keep them warm and provide a little light, but wasn't nearly as obvious as a fire, so they were in little danger of detection from any hostile forces. Dryce doubted they had much to worry about in this stretch of forest, but procedures were procedures.

When Dryce sat down he was sure to keep a little distance between himself and Peyton, making sure she understood that he would come no closer without an invitation. They couldn't avoid sleeping in the same quarters, but he would do his best to make her comfortable.

"For god's sake," Peyton said after several minutes of strained silence while they ate, "I said I was sorry. Stop fucking sulking. It was stupid, I told you that. And of the two of us, we clearly know which one is more likely to throw herself at the other."

Was he sulking? That seemed a little extreme. But Dryce didn't usually deal with rejection. When he singled out a partner, they were happy to spend the night with him, happy to embark on all the pleasures he wanted to share. Then again, he'd also encountered people who waved him off with a smile or a shake of their heads. And he'd never before done anything but shrug off the rejection.

But a rejection from Peyton was unthinkable. She was the one person in the entire universe meant for him. He'd traveled thousands of light years and only found her by some miracle. And yet she didn't know what she meant to him and he knew that if he told her now, she'd only run away. But *sulking* was not something a warrior should do, and Dryce would not stand for it any longer.

He summoned his best grin and leaned in until their shoulders almost brushed, the heat caught between them a living thing. "There's no need to throw yourself," he said. "But if you do, I'll be here to catch you."

Peyton dragged in a ragged breath and suddenly the air around them teemed with the promise of something more. Dryce realized that he'd been doing this all wrong. Giving his denya space was not the way to make her want him. No, she was strong and her mind as bright as a star. She needed to be challenged, needed to know she was wanted and given all of the evidence a scientist could wish for to prove it was true.

Dryce dropped his hand down and dragged the outer edge of his knuckle over her forearm and watched as she shivered. And she didn't pull away. "You'll always be safe with me," he promised. "And I'm right here. Any way you want me."

That seemed to break her out of her spell and she pulled away. "For now," she muttered.

No, they were done with that. Dryce opened his hand and placed it on her wrist, her pulse fluttering under his fingers. He didn't grasp hard enough to hold her in place, but she didn't yank out of his hold. "You are the only person I see, Peyton. I'm not looking for any other."

"So you're saying that your reputation is all talk?" The thread of hope in her voice could have driven him to his knees.

"I won't lie about my past," even if he now regretted parts of it. Not because it hadn't been fun, but because it made his denya doubt that he could want her and only her. "But it doesn't matter now."

"Why not?" Still she didn't pull her hand away, but tension thrummed under her skin, her muscles clenched tight enough to hurt.

Dryce froze, indecision stealing his voice. If she could not feel the bond between them, he didn't know how to make her believe in it. And if she turned from him now, he could compromise their entire mission by disrupting the fragile accord they'd managed to come to.

Peyton took his silence for something else and finally pulled her hand away. "I'm not looking for a hookup," she said, putting nearly a meter of distance between them. "So let's just pretend that we never kissed and this conversation never happened. Okay?"

She raised her eyebrows, waiting for him to agree. She would be waiting for a long time. Dryce's timing was terrible, but there was nothing about his mate he was willing to forget. Not ever.

***

The tent was suffocatingly hot despite the chill in the night outside. Peyton didn't sleep well, but she'd be lying if she tried to blame it on the heat. No, it all had to do with the hulking, way too sexy, hunk of alien muscle lying just out of reach of her fingertips. Not that she'd actually tried to reach out and touch him. That would make her the queen of mixed signals, feeling him up in the middle of the night after making it clear that nothing was going to happen between them.

God, she'd wanted so badly to believe him when he started spouting that bullshit about not looking at anyone but her. And then in his next breath he'd proved it was all a lie, and a line, something he was feeding her to make her let down her guard so she could be just another one of his conquests.

There were so many other Detyen warriors who could have joined up with her on his mission. Why had she been stuck with the one who made her burn?

Morning was a quiet affair, and Peyton was just happy to escape the cloying heat of the tent. It was difficult to believe that just a bit of fabric and two bodies could create a sauna like that, and she didn't look forward to the coming night. If anything, sleeping in tent had given her more motivation to get through this mission as quickly as she could. Once they were done she'd return to her own bed and never need to look at Dryce again.

She tried to tell herself that the pang in her chest at that thought was a happy feeling, but a yawning chasm of hollowness didn't really feel that way.

Maybe things wouldn't have seemed so dire if she could message DF, but even the thought of him wasn't enough to raise her spirits. And when she tried to imagine who he might be, a disturbingly desirable image began to form of a towering alien with bluish green skin and a killer smile.

"Any updates?" She forced her mind back on the job, plowing through a simple breakfast before packing up her share of the camp and storing it back on the helicopter.

"No," Dryce replied. "We're to proceed to the second location and use our discretion."

And after a week of meetings with the SDA and the Detyen Legion she understood exactly what that meant. If there were hostiles waiting, they were simply doing recon. If not, they'd do just what they'd done the day before and look for a bomb for her to defuse.

Peyton climbed into her seat and only realized as they were lifting off that she wasn't freaking out about the flight. Maybe it had to do with an entire day spent flying the day before. Or maybe it had to do with the fact that she trusted Dryce to get her safely to their location. She never would have expected that, but no matter what her personal issues were with the man, she knew he was exactly the warrior that any person should be glad to have by their side.

Location 2 was a few hours' flight away from their camp. Peyton sat back in her seat and watched the landscape under them rush by, almost enchanted by the lush leaves and beautiful colors of her home. She'd never known how magical Earth could look from above, and while her fears were being held at bay she wanted to enjoy it.

She and Dryce didn't talk, and the tension of the things not said, and the things they'd said the night before, hung in the air. She didn't know why she felt so bad about it all. Nothing she'd stated was false. He was a known player, someone with a new lover every night. Why should she think he wanted to change just for her?

Why should she care that he didn't have a good answer?

It wasn't like she wanted him. Okay, it wasn't like she wanted him out of anything but the most animalistic lust. That was something she could satisfy with anyone. Like DF, who was waiting for a date when she got back.

So why did it make her a little ill to think of anyone but Dryce?

Peyton wasn't going to think about that now. And if she had her way, she wouldn't think of it *ever*. She was going through some sort of weird transference, wondering romantically about DF while forced to spend all her time with Dryce. No wonder she was confused.

An alert beeped, startling her out of her unwanted thoughts. She sat up straighter in her seat and looked over to see Dryce with his eyes narrowed as he looked at the display.

"What is it?" she asked. There were hundreds of different warnings that the machine could give them, but Peyton only had the ones pertaining to mechanical failure memorized. Thankfully the series of beeps playing now didn't sound anything like that.

"We're picking up some unexpected comm waves. This close to our location and they might be from hostiles." Dryce was all business now, the flirt from last night gone in the wake of the serious job they had to do. "I'm running a more thorough check. We may need to divert to our secondary landing location."

Peyton nodded like her agreement had any effect on the situation. Dryce was the one who had to make these decisions, but right now she had no reason to argue. "How far out is the secondary location?" She'd studied the maps before they'd left, but the information had all tangled together in her mind and she couldn't recall all the details.

"Ten kilometers from the target. Any closer and the cloaking is liable to fail." Dryce didn't look at her while he spoke, his entire being focused on monitoring the alarms while he flew the helicopter.

"Is there anything I can do to help?" She hated to be useless, and sitting in the passenger seat and looking out the window while Dryce managed so many tasks made her wish she knew how to fly with any skill, just so she could take one responsibility away from him.

He pushed a monitor until it swiveled towards her. "Read that out when it comes in. And tell me if the number on that gauge goes over fifty-seven."

She did as she was told without asking why she was doing it. He could explain the finer details later. Right now she just had to deliver information as quickly and clearly as possible. In a handful of minutes the first report came in and Dryce's mouth tightened as she read out a stream of numbers and a list of information she didn't understand.

Give her an alien engine any day and she could piece it back together. What she was looking at now may as well have been Ancient Greek.

The helicopter jerked to the left and Peyton let out an undignified *eep* and clutched the sides of her seat before they righted themselves. Dryce muttered an apology but didn't spare her another thought. Peyton took several deep breaths, trying to get her suddenly roiling fears out of control. She'd hoped the panic would stay away, but, of course, a person didn't get over her fears in a day. She clutched the seat tight and did her best to bottle up her emotions. She'd deal with the fallout later.

Though her sweating palms and the sudden ice in her veins were not signs that her emotional control was working.

"Read me those numbers again," Dryce demanded, harsh enough to snap her out of her momentary fear.

She glared at him, but her expression softened when she saw only concern in his eyes. She'd bet all the money in her bank account that he didn't need the numbers again, he just wanted her to focus on something other than her fear. So she took a deep breath and told him the readings, and when he thanked her, she did her best to remain calm.

"Hostiles?" she finally asked, once the immediate flurry of sensors and readings had subsided.

He gave a half shrug and spared her a glance for a second before looking back out in front of them. "Someone's down there. No way to know exactly who until we are on the ground."

"Did this mission just get a lot more dangerous?" Because now she wasn't certain whether she wanted to keep flying in the death trap or land and hunt down the possibly armed aliens intent on destroying the planet.

"It was always dangerous," her companion reminded her. "But you've got me. No one out there stands a chance."

She should have laughed at his confidence, should have found it ridiculous. Instead all Peyton could do was smile and hold that reassurance close. For whatever reason, she was almost convinced when Dryce told her that no harm would come to her, and she'd much rather be by his side than stuck out here alone.

They had a job to do, and he was going to make sure that it got done.

Chapter Eleven

Something felt wrong from the moment Dryce and Peyton touched down. A feeling of expectation hung in the air around them, like at any moment things could explode and foil all of their plans. Ten kilometers sounded like a far enough distance when Dryce and the team had been making their plans, but now he wished they were a hundred kilometers away. He hated leading his mate into danger, hated that there could be hostile forces waiting for them at the other side of the forest, and there was nothing he could do but stand at Peyton's side and do his best to shield her from harm.

"Put this on." Dryce held out a vest he'd pulled from the storage compartment. It was thick, a little heavy, and embedded with several safety features that protected the wearer from blaster fire and other minor weapons.

Peyton studied the material then looked up at him. "A shield? Why aren't you wearing one?" She shucked off her jacket, put on the vest, then put her jacket back on.

"They can interfere with the electronics in the blasters. Makes shooting accurately impossible." And there was only one vest. Space on the helicopter was limited and protective gear could take up a lot of room. They had the basics, but a vest like what he'd given to Peyton was top of the line, not something doled out on every mission.

Peyton bit her lip and glanced down at the dark material. "If it interferes with electronics, I can't wear it while I'm doing my job." She reached for the hem as if to take it off, but Dryce held a hand up to stop her.

"Then take it off when you're working and put it back on after. I don't want you getting hit." Blaster fire wasn't usually fatal, but it hurt like all the hells and if he could save Peyton from any pain, he'd do whatever it took.

His denya didn't mention how dangerous it would be to stand in hostile territory without the vest, but he could see the thoughts spinning through her mind. He packed up his gear and Peyton took what she could, but they traveled light. The hike to the site would take some time, but they'd be back at the helicopter by dark, and they didn't plan to take much back with them after they investigated.

The hike wasn't silent, though they didn't do much speaking. Birds chirped and the wind rustled through the leaves, but still Dryce felt that something was wrong. He wanted this mission to be over as soon as possible, but there was no way to finish it without possibly engaging with hostiles. Normally he'd look forward to battle, but not while he walked at his denya's side.

He didn't know how Raze did it. Sierra was out there somewhere with the team and she could just as easily be cut down as any of them. Raze would lay down his life before he let that happen, but sometimes losses couldn't be prevented.

"Are you okay?" Peyton asked, laying her hand gently on his arm. She tipped her head up at him, eyes wide as she studied his expression.

Dryce didn't know what he was giving away, but he couldn't focus on the things that could go wrong with his brother. He was distracted enough focusing on keeping Peyton safe. Worrying about things he couldn't control would only split his focus and make things worse.

"I'm fine," he replied, wincing as the lie passed his lips. A person didn't lie to their denya, not like this, and it wounded his soul to do something even so minor. And it only compounded the hurt he was feeling from keeping the other half of his identity from her.

Peyton narrowed her eyes. "I don't think you are." She spoke quietly, just as aware as him of the danger they could be in at any moment.

Dryce could lie again, but he sensed that would lead to an argument, and they'd already argued enough. Besides, if he was going to concentrate on their surroundings, it was better to get out the other side of this conversation as quickly as possible than to keep evading. He sighed and scanned their surroundings by habit before answering. There was no one but them and the forest, no sense of hostile forces at all.

"My brother is on this mission with his denya. I don't know how he does it. She is in just as much danger as him, and it must be driving him crazy." Because if it wasn't, Dryce desperately needed to ask him for advice on how to make it through.

"Denya?" Peyton asked, brows scrunched in question.

"His mate. They've been together since just before we all came to this planet." If he could avoid it, he wasn't going to explain the denya bond or the denya price, not right now. If *this* conversation was distracting, he could only imagine how bad it would be to explain that he'd die at the age of thirty if Peyton wouldn't claim him.

"That's not very long," she replied after a loaded moment of silence.

"Time is irrelevant when it comes to the denya bond. Raze has walked out into danger with the only person in the universe meant to be by his side, the one he is bound to protect. I do not like to think on what he's going though." Would it be easier or harder if he and Peyton were fully mated? At least he could be sure of her then, be sure that she wanted to be by his side and share in his hardships. But he'd heard stories of what it felt like to be truly mated, truly bound, and he couldn't imagine what it would be like to risk that connection to enemy fire.

"She's a soldier, right?" Peyton clambered over a fallen tree branch and almost tripped when she made it to the other side. "It was the talk of the office for at least a week when you all showed up, and we talked a little when we were preparing for the mission."

Soldier. Spy. Close enough in this case. Dryce nodded.

"Then she's probably not happy about the thought of being left behind," Peyton pointed out. "I'm not exactly jumping for joy being out here, but I belong in a lab. If I'd trained for years and then some guy was telling me that I couldn't do my work because it's dangerous, I'd slap him upside the head and talk some sense into him. Or kick him to the curb. Whichever's easiest. They might be fated to be together or whatever, but that doesn't mean that their training and responsibility is just going to disappear."

Logically, that all made sense. But the denya bond had nothing to do with logic.

"Let me guess," she continued, tossing a grin at him as if this was all hypothetical. "If you could manage to restrain yourself to a single mate, you'd keep her locked up in a padded room and only allowed out when the building was secured by no less than five—no, ten!—warriors." She rolled her eyes and shook her head as if she could imagine this scenario she'd conjured up.

Dryce looked at the forest around them and glanced back at Peyton. Now would be a moment to tell her. If only to prove that he would never try and stop his mate from being herself. "I would have no trouble 'restraining' myself to a single mate." He shot her a pointed look, but Peyton seemed able to brush it off with a shrug.

"Are you sure? No more clubs? No more groupies?" She laughed, but there was a serious question in her eyes, as if she didn't want the answer to matter as much as it did.

"No one but my denya." Dryce stopped walking as he said it, turning fully toward Peyton and giving her the full weight of his gaze. "I haven't sat idly by waiting for the day I

161

recognize my mate, but once I'm hers, I will seek no others."

What use was a promise if she didn't know he was making it to her?

"Peyton—"

A crack echoed around them, a tree branch snapping and crashing through the trees. Dryce pushed Peyton behind him and raised his blaster, ready for trouble from any direction. They moved forward carefully, but when they got to the fallen branch, there was nothing to suggest that it had succumbed to anything but the wind. Still, they walked more carefully and this time in the utmost quiet. Sound could carry strangely in the woods, and Dryce didn't want to alert any potential hostiles to their presence, especially not just so he could confess his feelings. There would be time for that later.

***

Peyton's gaze kept snagging on Dryce as they covered the last kilometer to their destination. Tension thrummed through her with every step they took, a confusing mix of emotions from what he'd said to her and the fear that the enemy could be lurking behind every tree branch.

For a second back there she'd been convinced that Dryce was going to confess something massive. Something she wasn't sure she could believe, and something she feared that she wanted more than she ever would have expected. But how could she want to be the playboy's mate?

If she hadn't been so worried about tipping off whatever enemy lay in wait, Peyton would have cursed. She couldn't wait to get back to the real world, and that had only a little bit to do with the amount of danger she and Dryce were in. She needed to be around people that *weren't* the hopelessly sexy warrior that had taken up residence in her mind and tempted her closer and closer to sin with each passing minute. Sure, he said he'd be satisfied with a single mate, just like her father had said he'd be happy with a life on Earth. People didn't change, not something as fundamental as that. She shouldn't be hoping that Dryce belonged to her. She should be grateful that he wasn't trying to.

They found a spot to observe the location from and once he was satisfied, Dryce handed a set of binoculars to her. Luckily whatever her vest did to deflect blasters didn't seem to affect the electronics of the binoculars and she was able to take a look. Unlike their last location, this one had clearly seen recent activity. There wasn't a road, but on the far side of the central building there was a break in the trees where it looked like some of the foliage had been cleared away. It wouldn't be difficult for a vehicle in hover mode to make it through that.

And the building itself was a bit of a hint that something was up. They were far away from civilization, hours by ground from the nearest major city, and the map she'd looked at only listed a few towns within a hundred kilometers. This area had mostly gone back to nature over the last century and the people who'd once called it home were long gone. But the building in front of them wasn't old, not as old as the remaining towns around here. No, it looked like a small warehouse or garage and couldn't have been around for more than a year or two. The forest ate things up quickly out here, and unless it was constantly maintained by whoever owned it, the animals and trees would have already been working to destroy it.

A gentle hum in the air tickled Peyton's ears and she shifted the binoculars until she found what she expected. "They've got generators," she said. It was the easiest way to maintain power in a place like this, but they were useless for stealth. Even the quietest generator hummed loud enough to be heard across a clearing when there were no other noises to drown it out.

Dryce took the binoculars back when she handed them over and looked where she pointed. He made a humming sound and took in a few more things before packing up the binoculars and pulling out a small tablet that fit in the palm of his hand, the holographic display hovering in the air between them and quickly mapping out the area around them.

"Trackers aren't picking up any activity," Dryce whispered as the holo display rotated around the camp, showing them different angles of the building in front of them. "Generator looks to be on standby."

From sound alone, Peyton could agree on that point. "They shut off automatically after twenty-four hours in standby mode," she said. "So that probably means someone was here recently."

"Or they turned them on remotely and they're coming back," he suggested.

Peyton shivered; she didn't want unexpected company. "Can your tracker get a look inside the building?"

Dryce shook his head, expression intense. "Only a basic reading, no images. If we want to see inside, we need to do it ourselves."

Wonderful. "What about surveillance?"

At that Dryce gave her his signature grin and Peyton was no less susceptible to it as the first time she'd seen it. "The trackers have two functions. Once I send the command they send out a short wave pulse. It will scramble all surveillance for about an hour and should appear to anyone watching to come from natural interference."

Depending on what the building looked like inside, they could need much more than an hour to explore, but they'd take what they could get. Dryce led the way after pressing a command on the tablet. The holo display disappeared as the function of the trackers switched over from observation to obfuscation. Breaking cover of the trees was the most nerve wracking experience that Peyton could remember. She expected a shot to come at them at any second, but it became clearer and clearer that she and Dryce were the only two people there.

So what was someone using this place for? The construction looked human, but she wouldn't have known how to identify Wreetan or Oscavian architecture. They were on Earth, though, so whatever the enemy had built had most likely come from the planet.

As they turned the corner, they saw a large garage door and a smaller entrance beside it. There was no door covering the opening, and Dryce approached it slowly, weapon drawn and ready to engage with any threat. But still none came.

He got close to the door and looked ready to step through it, but before he could cross the threshold, Peyton put an arm on his shoulder and yanked him back. He was made of muscle and outweighed her by enough to count, but the warning was enough to stop him.

He shot her a questioning look.

Peyton bent over and picked up a small branch on the ground and chucked it at the door. It gave off a wicked spark as it smoked and fell down to the ground outside the door. "Force field." They weren't common on building entrances, but she'd seen plenty used to guard precious artifacts that she was supposed to work on. It had only taken burning her hands a few times for her to learn to recognize them by sight and the faint hint of ozone they gave off.

"Can you disable it?" Dryce asked. He stared at the opening like the door could offer the answers of the universe. But it was just a simple force field, it had no answers to give.

"The controls are liable to be inside, so no." Peyton hated not to use her skills, but there was only so much she could do. "Taking out the generators *might* work, but that could have an alarm on it and could call down whoever owns this place. Even then, a force field like this if it's properly set up runs on an independent power source. The best way in is to find another door."

That proved difficult. Beside the force field guarded entrance and the locked garage door, there wasn't a way inside. The windows they found were too high up for them to reach, even with Peyton climbing on Dryce's shoulders, and time was running out.

They tried forcing the garage door open, but it was locked and the door was so huge, taking up nearly a third of the tall outer wall, that even if they'd managed to unlock it, she wasn't certain that she and Dryce could lift it up.

Meanwhile, Peyton's mind was spinning, trying to work out the puzzle of the open entrance. She played with the edge of the vest Dryce had forced her to wear and encountered a small bit of wire sewn into the hem. Probably part of the system to defray blaster fire.

Well, that could work.

"How important is it to keep our presence a secret?" she asked, practically bouncing from foot to foot as her mind worked out the puzzle, putting the pieces into place and making them fit with wire and ingenuity.

Dryce studied her with narrowed eyes. "Why?"

"I think I can get us inside, but it will be obvious someone tampered with the door. We can probably disguise it with a fallen tree branch, but if anyone looks closely, they might realize that we did something." Her fingers were already moving, ready to grab her toolkit and get them in, but she needed Dryce's okay.

"How fast can you get us in?"

"Five minutes?" If this worked she'd only need two, if it didn't work, the time didn't matter. Dryce gave a nod and Peyton grinned. She pulled out a small cloth wallet that contained a spool of copper wire and some of her finer tools and then stripped off her coat and the protective vest. Dryce let out a small sound of protest, but once she started stripping the fabric off the vest he subsided. She yanked out the power source and got to work.

After a minute Peyton looked up at him, a small drill in her mouth. "How important was that tablet you were using earlier?" She held out her hand, needing one of the components that was sure to be inside.

"I have a spare," Dryce handed over the tablet and waited.

It wasn't easy to set up, and she'd only have one shot, but once Peyton was satisfied that things were as good as they were going to get, she got as close to the entrance as she dared and tossed her coiled ball of wires and electronics at the door and held her breath.

The device exploded.

Dryce tackled her to the ground, covering her body with his own and shielding her from whatever was coming towards them, but after a moment there was no more excitement and the smell of burning electronics surrounded them. Dryce pulled back and Peyton smiled up at him. "I think it worked."

"You didn't say anything about an explosion." He tried to keep his face serious, but a smile threatened at the corners of his mouth.

"All good science comes with a risk of explosions," Peyton informed him. She wanted to pull him down and kiss him in triumph. It wasn't bomb defusing, but she'd found a challenge that only she could meet and she'd succeeded. Dryce rolled back and offered her a hand up. Peyton took it gladly and they walked into the building.

There was nothing much to see inside, and she choked a bit on the smoke from her improvised force field key.

Dryce pulled something out of one of his pockets and set it on the ground.

"What's that?"

"Recorder. We don't have much time, but it should be able to get a full picture before we leave." He rolled the device away and Peyton watched as it moved around them, silently taking in the room.

From the inside it seemed impossibly large, as if the true scale had been hidden while they were standing outside. Catwalks ringed an upper floor but left a large area completely bare from floor to ceiling, and rutted tracks in the cement floor suggested that something heavy had been moved at some point.

Peyton and Dryce walked the place, but there was no bomb, and it seemed like it was all for naught.

Until Peyton found the barrels.

"Fuck." She recognized the smell from several meters away and raised her hand to cover her mouth and noise. That shit was toxic as hell and she didn't want her or Dryce breathing in more of it than necessary.

But she had to be sure.

As a precaution she'd brought a sample kit with her. She could perform basic chemical compound scans and had several secure vials that could be used to transport samples. She didn't want to get any closer to the barrels, but she didn't have a choice.

Dryce was immediately at her side. "What is it?"

"Not good." The kit she carried came with a pair of gloves, but the thin material wouldn't offer much protection from the corrosive chemical. Still, she put them on. Negligible protection was better than no protection at all. "If I'm right this is a really dirty accelerant that could be used in a bomb. Three barrels of it is more than enough for just about anything, and judging by the state of this warehouse, I'd guess this is excess." She moved as quickly and carefully as she could, scraping a sample from around the opening of the barrel, not willing to risk opening. She got a basic reading from her scanner which seemed to confirm her suspicions.

Something near Dryce beeped and he looked at his communicator. "We need to get out of here. Time's almost up."

Peyton secured her sample and was thankful to step back from the chemicals. Dryce found his recorder and they made their way outside. It took a few moments to find a tree branch that they could set up to look like it had battered the force field enough to overpower it, but they set the scene and were out of the warehouse just in time.

A vehicle came through the trees almost silently, the loudest sound coming from where its body smacked against the wood. The garage door opened with a creak and the vehicle slid inside, the door closing behind it without anyone getting out to check out the damaged entrance.

"Did you get a look at them?" Peyton asked. She hadn't managed to see anything beside the vague outlines of the passengers.

Dryce shook his head. "We need to leave. Now."

Chapter Twelve

They had enough time to head to the third location, but Dryce pulled them out almost before they began. His sensors were going crazy, warning of hostiles nearby and recording a variety of weapons that had no place in a peaceful forest on Earth. He sent out his drones in stealth mode and he and Peyton waited in anxious silence at the helicopter. They couldn't risk letting the drones transmit data directly back to his tablet, so it was more than two hours before they could leave. He stashed the drones away and they were off, heading back towards DC and away from whoever was causing trouble in the middle of these woods.

"You're not going to analyze the data?" Peyton asked as Dryce lifted off. He hadn't even bothered to extract the data stores from the drones. That would be for the team once they got back.

"They're sure to be on high alert after we checked out the second location. I don't want you caught." He didn't realize that he'd said it that way until Peyton's breath stuttered.

"I—" He could see her shaking her head out of the corner of his eye. "I can't say I'll be disappointed to sleep in my own bed tonight." That hadn't been what she was going to say at first, he was sure of it, but he didn't press. They were on the mission now, that was what had to come first.

"We'll be back," Dryce promised. "And with a bigger team. We should have had more than just distant support since this started, but they wanted us moving fast and light." And with a civilian, that had been one of the most dangerous decisions that Dryce had ever seen Sandon and the rest of the Detyen leadership make.

"Fate of the world," Peyton replied, almost like she'd read his mind. "We don't have the luxury of waiting around."

The flight back to headquarters was tense, with Dryce on high alert waiting for any signs of hostile pursuit. Once he was certain they were out of range of any surveillance he contacted their base and informed them of the change of plans.

Peyton sat beside him, hands clenched into fists, but Dryce didn't know what to say to calm her down. The mission had changed, their time alone together had suddenly come to an end, and no matter what he felt about that, she was sure to be happy. He didn't want the reminder that she couldn't stand him outside of the times she wanted to kiss him.

"What comes next?" she asked, breaking the silence after nearly an hour. At least now the tension in the air didn't come from their strained relationship but from the threat of Oscavians and Wreetans hellbent on destroying their home.

Dryce glanced over and offered a quick smile. "We regroup. Plan a more careful breach of the third location, and once we're satisfied, we'll head back out. Hopefully the drones caught sight of whatever it is they're building. They didn't have long to scan, but they're powerful little beasties."

Her lips pulled into something that might have been a grin at the mention of the machines. "I know," she confessed, "I was part of the team that designed them."

"Really?" He'd been amazed by the dexterity of that piece of tech when the humans showed it to him, but no one had said a word about Peyton working on them.

"We scavenged something like them off a pirate vessel that was recovered on Mars. I reverse engineered the drone and suggested some design changes that would make it work better on Earth. They're not exactly cheap, but I know that field agents have been happy with them." She said it simply, as if it wasn't amazing that a person could take tech from another planet, another civilization that shared no common roots with her own, and figure out how it worked and then improve on it.

Dryce wanted to hear more, he wanted to know the inner workings of his denya's mind. She fascinated him and captivated him, and if he'd been slightly less concerned with the safety of the Detyen and human races he might have diverted their helicopter and stolen away with her to a place no one would be able to find them.

"What else have you worked on?" he asked instead.

And Peyton *bloomed*. Her smile grew wide, but she didn't speak immediately, instead taking several moments to think. And then her grin grew impossibly bigger and she started to talk, her hands waving as she explained her current project, a cloaking mechanism recovered from another craft that had crashed in upstate New York. "We don't normally have a problem with pirates, but the past few years we've seen a flurry of activity. It's terrible for people who get scared, or abducted, but the tech we're seeing is unbelievable. The day could be twice as long and I still wouldn't have enough time to get through everything in my lab."

Some of the things she mentioned, Dryce hadn't realized weren't common on Earth, but other improvements and modifications she'd implemented blew his mind. The woman might have been afraid of flight, but the ships leaving the planet had a lot to thank her and her team for.

Because every time she told him about something she'd discovered, she was sure to give credit to the rest of her people for their parts, insisting that the work she did was impossible to do alone.

"Did you start working on things from space to feel closer to your dad?" Dryce asked as she told him about her first solo project in college.

And the happy expression was gone from Peyton's face. "What? What do you know about my dad?"

If the helicopter hadn't been mostly on automatic controls at this point, Dryce would have crashed as he scrambled to think of a reason to know about her family. She'd told him about her parent's marital problems and her father's wanderlust in their communicator messages, but she had no idea that she'd been talking to him. "Your file," Dryce finally muttered. "It said your dad was a space pilot." Probably, it *probably* said that, but Dryce hadn't read the entire thing.

"My file?" she responded cautiously, eyes narrowed. "What else did this file say?"

He stood on the edge of a cliff and she was ready to push him off with one wrong word. How could Dryce be so *stupid*? They'd been doing well. She'd been opening up, and he'd gotten to see just how brilliant a woman fate had seen fit to choose for him. And now he had to dash all hope to pieces because he couldn't keep his identities straight.

He needed to come clean. Needed to tell her that she'd been talking to him for weeks now, that she'd shared secrets with him that she didn't tell anyone else. He needed to tell her that she was his mate and he wanted to spend all of his days showing her that they were better when they were together. This part of the mission was over, it wouldn't put much in jeopardy to confess.

But Dryce didn't want to do it yet. He'd started to formulate a plan and a half-assed confession on a flight home from an aborted mission had no place in it.

"It said you're brilliant. Best mech the SDA has to offer." That part was true. And he didn't want to say much more out of concern that he'd reveal too much.

"Yeah, fine," Peyton subsided, slouching back in her seat. "But my dad has nothing to do with it. I'm good because I worked my ass off and I love what I do, I don't do it for the approval of some—ugh!" She shook her head and turned away, staring out the window and saying no more.

Dryce didn't try to make her talk. He'd done enough damage already.

***

Peyton couldn't get off of the helicopter fast enough. The last stretch of the ride crawled on, but when they set down she was off like a shot, not even giving Dryce a chance to say goodbye. She was sure someone would insist on talking to her, *debriefing* her, or whatever the right word for it was, but she needed a few minutes alone. After two days in Dryce's constant company, she was going to go crazy if she couldn't take ten freaking seconds to unwind.

Though, strangely enough, being around him full time hadn't actually bothered her until he dropped that shit about her dad. Was her family's entire sordid history laid out for anyone with security clearance to read about?

No. No, it couldn't be. Why would it?

Oh, shit. She'd completely overreacted.

Peyton found a bathroom and hid, locking the door behind her and sliding down the wall to sit on the tile floor, heedless of the germs. Sure, she was afraid of heights, but germs had never bothered her that much. That was what soap and water was for.

She sucked in a deep breath, her noise itching from the astringent scent of whatever cleaner had been recently used. Things didn't normally hit her like this. Yeah, she knew she was a bit screwed up from the way her dad had abandoned the family and then unceremoniously died, but she was nearly thirty years old, she hadn't had a father for more than half of her life, she should be able to deal with that. One innocent question from a co-worker shouldn't send her over the edge.

Hell, she'd been able to tell DF the entire story without freaking out! Though, if she thought about it, she'd been able to confess all of that to him because they were basically strangers. She didn't need to worry about his judgment, didn't need to examine the look in his eyes as she confessed that her father hadn't loved his family enough to stay on the planet where he belonged.

"Get a grip, girl," she muttered, slowly standing up and making her way to the sink. A look in the mirror made her grimace. She was dirty, like she'd just spent two days running through the forest beside a massive warrior that she wanted to climb like a tree when she wasn't pissed at him. Her dark eyes were tired and hollow, and she only had Dryce to blame for that.

No, that wasn't fair. It was her own issues that were to blame, he'd just triggered them.

She splashed some water on her face, and while it couldn't do much to fix the hollow look, it did get rid of the dirt and woke her up a bit. Once she dried off, she pulled out her communicator and turned it on for the first time since they'd left. Maybe that wasn't the proper protocol, but she needed a little slice of normalcy. She was a bit disappointed, and strangely relieved, to see that DF hadn't contacted her. Other than to tell her that he would *definitely* be interested in a date when she was back, he'd been silent, just as she'd requested.

There was, however, a series of messages from Ella, growing more and more insistent over the last three days when Peyton had gone completely dark. She rolled her eyes at the urgency of her sister's messages. It wasn't like she'd disappeared without a trace. She'd explained that work was taking her off the grid for up to a week and she'd be in touch when she got back. But Peyton was still reeling from those memories of her dad and she realized that she wasn't the only surviving member of her family who might have some issues associated with someone leaving for work with little explanation.

Peyton: Calm down, kiddo! Job isn't over yet, but I'm on a break.

Ella: Where have you BEENNNNNNN??????????

Peyton: At work, drama queen. What's up?

Ella: Eh, just bored. Come over.

Peyton rolled her eyes. Typical Ella, everything was an emergency until she got attention, then it turned out she was just looking to pass the time.

Peyton: Sorry, no can do. Call your friends. Gotta go.

Ella: Boo! See if I throw you a birthday party next month.

Peyton: I'll be heartbroken. Talk to you later.

She shut off her communicator before Ella could drag her into anymore conversation. She knew it wouldn't take much to have her spilling the goods on Dryce and DF, and while she could get away with talking about her mysterious messenger, there were probably security reasons she shouldn't mention Dryce. And the fact that her sister was a total alien groupie. She did *not* want to find out that Dryce was one of Ella's conquests. Or the other way around. However that worked. No. No way.

Though, that *would* go a long way to erasing the weird attraction she couldn't seem to get over. Nothing cleared that up better than knowing the guy had slept with her sister.

She almost powered her comm back on just to confirm that he hadn't. But that was crossing a line that Peyton didn't want to admit she was getting close to, and she had no reason to believe that the two of them knew each other or *knew* each other. Not in any meaning of the word. Hell, DF had a better chance of knowing her sister, seeing as he was at that bar the night she'd lost her communicator. Gross, no, she didn't want to consider that.

If her conversation with Ella did one thing, it was calm her nerves enough to give Peyton the strength to go back outside and face the debrief and Dryce. She wanted this mission to be over, she wanted the Earth to be a safe place again, and she wanted to be able to forget the sexy alien who'd wormed his way into her thoughts and had already burrowed so deep that she wasn't sure she'd be able to excise him without hurting herself.

But first she had to finish the mission, and they weren't done yet.

Chapter Thirteen

Iris had practically worn a hole in the floor over the last two days. Her nails were bit down to the quick and if she didn't have news soon, she was scared she might start pulling out her hair. And all of this because her mate was on a *support* mission. She hated to think what she'd be like if he had to go out to fight. No, she could imagine. They'd probably need to sedate her.

After a month of mated bliss it was like the real world had come crashing down on her. Hard. She knew her mate was a warrior, knew he had duties to his people that he could not ignore. But it was easy to forget when his days were spent in training sessions and meetings with his fellow Detyens and the humans at the Sol Defense Agency.

But with the apprehension of Brakley Varrow things had sped up. And Iris shuddered to think of that man. His brother had been bad enough, and if it were up to her, both of the Varrows would have been consigned to hell without a second thought. More strategic minds than hers were the ones in charge, though, and with the Oscavian warships getting closer by the day, battle was no longer a possibility, it was only a matter of when.

But Iris needed to see Toran. She wanted to hate this needy feeling within, wanted to ball it up and throw it into a deep hole with all her other unpleasant emotions, but if it was the cost for the soaring highs of loving him, she'd take it. There was nothing on Earth, nothing in the galaxy that would make her give him up, not now that she'd found him. She'd never realized just how perfect a match she could have, what it was like to engage with someone mentally, physically, and emotionally so completely that sometimes it was like they were one being split into two parts.

And right now one half of that whole was crying out for its other half, and she just wanted Toran home. Now.

She heard the lock engage and her head snapped up, her eyes watching the door open slowly with the desperation of a starving person watching meat sizzle on a grill. A flash of gold skin was all she needed to see before she sprinting across the rooms and wrapping her arms tightly around her mate, holding on almost hard enough to cut off his airflow.

But Toran didn't seem to mind. He held on just as tightly, his big hands a familiar presence on her back, the warmth of him suffusing her, heating her even though she hadn't realized that she'd been cold.

Someone observing them would have thought they hadn't seen each other for months, maybe *years*, rather than the span of a weekend, but since their mating they'd spent every night together and this was the first time Toran had been called away, the first time that danger was a real possibility.

A cool burst of air ruffled her hair and Iris realized that the door was hanging open with them embracing for anyone to see. Iris's cheeks flamed as she realized someone would have been treated to quite the view if things had gone on for a few more minutes. She untangled herself from Toran's grip and shut the door, engaging the lock and sealing them off from the rest of the world.

"Is the mission over?" she asked. He'd said it would be a week or more, so it was hard to believe that he'd come home so soon, no matter how much she wanted it. "You didn't sneak away, did you?" The thought of being wanted that much was humbling, but she didn't want her mate shirking his duties and putting others in danger just to see her. Well, *most* of her didn't want that, but the needy part who'd paced ten kilometers in her small house was jumping for joy at the thought.

Toran tipped her chin up and kissed her, obliterating all thoughts as his tongue tangled with hers, giving her the taste of home she'd come to associate with him. She couldn't believe how tangled up together they'd gotten in the past month, but she wouldn't have it any other way.

Her mate finally pulled away to respond, even as she chased him for another taste. "There was a bit of a complication. I'll need to go back out again shortly, but they've given us the night to rest."

"Huh?" Why was he talking when they could be kissing? Oh, it took Iris's brain a moment to catch up to the fact that he was answering her question. "What kind of complication? Was anyone hurt?" His entire team had been involved and she knew how much he cared for them all. It would weigh heavily on him if anything were to happen to them.

"No," he said to her relief. "We had multiple locations to scout and one of them was too hot to get close to." His hands landed on her hips and he pulled her close until she could feel every centimeter of him. Every *hard* centimeter of him. "Now, do you really want to know all about the mission? Or was there something else you wanted?"

Iris moaned as his fingers found their way under her blouse and made contact with her naked flesh. "You can tell me the rest later," she managed to get out before she crushed her mouth over his and hooked her legs around his hips. He could tell her all about the mission later, but right now she needed him to show her just what they'd been missing by being apart. She'd need it if he was about to go back into the field.

***

Toran and Kayde had made themselves scarce the moment that Sandon cleared the team to leave, but Raze had surprised Dryce by volunteering to go with him to observe this meeting. Then again, Raze was the only member of the team who hadn't recently been separated from his denya, and while Dryce was sure they'd be all over one another the moment they were behind closed doors, it probably gave Raze and Sierra a little more self-control than the rest of the team.

Dryce envied them all. He hadn't known what kind of torture it could be to be so close to his denya and yet be unable to touch her. If anything, their kiss had only made it worse. Now whenever he closed his eyes, and sometimes while his mind simply wandered, he could remember the taste of her, the press of her lips against his, and he hungered for more, for anything and everything she could give to him. Could she not feel the burning pulse of need that he did? How could the denya bond affect him so strongly and leave her immune?

Maybe he would have posed these questions to his brother, but where they were standing at the moment was no place to think of the kinder emotions.

Brakley Varrow sat in the middle of a dark room, his hands bound behind his back and his ankles shackled to his chair. His formerly bright purple skin had taken on a sickly gray tinge and his dark hair was greasy and in desperate need of a wash. His bright blue eyes, however, remained defiant. Since his failed escape attempt after he'd been apprehended, he'd offered the SDA and the Detyen Legion no information. He seemed confident that Yormas of Wreet would prevail in the coming battle and rescue Varrow before the planet was destroyed.

The Oscavian who'd been captured at the same time wasn't so sure. It had taken him some time to crack, but now he was talking and the SDA interrogators were ready to use their new information to see if Varrow had anything he wanted to share.

When Dryce heard that the interview was happening, he'd put in a request to observe. If there was any information that would tell them how to find or disarm the weapons that were waiting somewhere on the planet and promising

Earth's destruction, he wanted to know. And he wanted to know it as soon his possible. His family, his friends, and his mate all called this place home and now Dryce did too. He wasn't ready to see his new home destroyed and if he could do anything to prevent the kind of pain that lived within the surviving Detyen people, he would do it.

But every time Varrow spoke, Dryce wanted to punch him. His tone was slimy, slippery, like he believed that if he just found the right set of words he'd be able to talk his way out of any situation. He said he was a simple scientist with no military knowledge, but Dryce could tell the man was hiding things from his past, and it wasn't just because he had an Oscavian fleet under his command.

Or he *had* before he'd been captured.

Now Yormas of Wreet controlled it all, and he was showing no signs of a willingness to retrieve his captured partner.

"How long do you think it will take him to crack?" Dryce asked. The SDA interrogators had been speaking to Varrow for more than an hour, but the Oscavian had done little more than twitch since they'd started asking questions. He seemed nervous, like he expected violence, but the SDA didn't use torture. Not unless asking questions nonstop, until it felt like each one hit with the crack of a whip, counted.

"I'm not sure he will," Raze replied with narrowed eyes. He was staring at Varrow hard enough that the man should have spontaneously combusted, but Varrow didn't even know that either of them were there. "From what Laurel has said about him, he's not exactly the most… sane. He very well might choose to die on this planet rather than save himself by telling us where the weapons are."

"He's dead either way. Dead or stuck in a cell for the rest of his life." Perhaps there was nothing crazy about making that choice, but Dryce wanted to grind his teeth together in frustration. "This is pointless. He's not going to talk." He pushed away from the observation post and spun on his heel, knocking on the door and signaling that he wanted to be let out. The door opened and Dryce was through it before the guard could completely step out of the way and Raze followed close on his heels.

They walked in silence through the dreary halls of the sub-basement in a building where the SDA kept their highest value prisoners. The whole place stank of desperation and despair and Dryce couldn't stand waiting there for another minute. He needed fresh air.

When he made it outside, the sun nearly blinded him. Still, he tilted his head up and soaked it in.

"What is it you really want, brother?" Raze asked after several moments. He stood off to the side of Dryce, out of his direct line of sight, as if he was afraid to spook him. It was something he would have never thought to do in the three years that he was soulless, and Dryce was thankful for the reminder that he had his brother back, even if he didn't want to discuss his problems at the moment.

What he really wanted, the *only* thing he wanted, was somewhere in the administration building and getting ready to go back to her home. And he'd walked out of their debrief without more than a bland farewell. Dryce kept screwing up, saying the wrong things, doing the wrong things, but maybe this was the worst of all. Putting this space between them only gave her more time to convince herself that he was made of wholly bad qualities and that he'd never be the right man for her.

For the first time he had the opportunity to show her who he was when he was off the job and able to give her all his attention. They had until morning to relax and recuperate before being sent out again. And if he didn't take this chance he could end up regretting it for the rest of his life, which was growing shorter by the hour.

He pulled out his communicator and smiled at his brother. "I know what I want. I have to go."

Chapter Fourteen

It took Peyton about fifteen minutes to crack and turn her phone back on. In her defense, she did it so she could call a taxi to come pick her up and take her home. But as soon as the screen came up she saw the message from DF and her heart flipped over.

DF: Can we meet tonight? There's something I need to tell you. I'm on the SDA base if you're around.

He was *here*? Peyton's head shot up and looked around for anyone that could be DF, but she was standing in the lobby of the admin building and plenty of people were milling around. All she knew was that DF was Detyen, so he could have been anyone that wasn't human in the building. That didn't exactly narrow it down.

Did she want to meet him now? She had to look horribly sleep deprived and her outfit was far more functional than cute. If she'd had time to plan a date, she would have allowed at least an hour to get ready to make sure she could look her best. Could she run home, change clothes, put on makeup, and make it back before it got ridiculously late? With traffic, probably not, and if she made DF wait too long he'd probably lose interest in meeting tonight. She checked the timestamp and saw that thirty minutes had already passed from when he'd sent the message. What if he'd already headed home?

Peyton: Can you meet in the cafeteria in fifteen minutes?

Her hands shook as she typed out the message. It was really going to happen. She was going to meet the mysterious stranger that she'd been messaging for weeks. The mystery would finally be solved and she might finally get to see where things were going to go between them.

Or it would all be a giant letdown and she wouldn't have anything to look forward to after the end of her mission. Except the survival of the planet. That was ultimately a good thing, she supposed.

DF: Yes, that's great.

DF: If you're surprised, give me a chance.

Peyton's eyebrows scrunched up at that ominous request. *If* she was surprised? She wanted to message back and demand what he meant, but she was going to see the guy for the first time in fifteen minutes. She could ask him what the hell he was talking about once they were face to face.

But would it be the first time? *If.* Surprised. They were anonymous message buddies, why would surprise come into it at all? Unless they already knew each other outside of that context. But Peyton could list the number of Detyens she knew beyond a passing acquaintance on one hand. And only one of them was single.

Dryce.

Oh god, it was Dryce, wasn't it?

She stumbled and had to catch herself on the wall before her body could crumble and collapse back to the floor. Dryce Na*Feen*. DF. It wasn't an exact match, but it was close.

He'd known about her dad. Had that only been this morning? But if Dryce and DF were one and the same, then Dryce hadn't snatched that information from a file somewhere, he'd known it because she'd told it to him. And if Dryce was DF, then he'd known who she was since the moment they'd met in person, but had kept that from her for some reason.

Some powerful emotion washed over her and Peyton couldn't tell whether it was good or bad. But it propelled her towards the cafeteria and she walked with such intensity that everyone in her path got out of her way when they caught sight of the look in her eyes.

It never occurred to her to turn around and go home, or to text DF and tell him the meeting was off. If he was Dryce, she needed to know. She needed to know if the weird companionship she'd felt with the Detyen Legion's biggest playboy had been some sort of fluke or if it came from the fact that they'd been developing a friendship over their communicators for weeks.

And then she needed to know why he'd lied to her.

She was going to yell herself hoarse demanding those answers.

The automatic doors to the cafeteria slid open, but Peyton wished that they were the kind you had to push. She needed to hit something, and the fewer inanimate objects in her way, the more likely it was that she was going to hit Dryce.

He was big, he could take a shove.

But she had no idea what she was going to do after that. Hug him? Kill him? Kick him? Kiss him? Climb him?

And what if it wasn't Dryce?

That thought stopped her in her tracks and she stood in the entrance of the cafeteria momentarily consumed with such a swell of disappointment that she didn't know how to process it. Did she *want* DF to be Dryce?

Oh hell, she wanted DF to be Dryce.

Now that she was in the cafeteria, Peyton wasn't sure where she was supposed to go. They hadn't set up a meeting location, almost as if they'd assumed they'd know one another on sight. She walked a little further into the room so she didn't block the entrance and grabbed the nearest table before settling down to watch the doors like a hawk. It wasn't near any specific meal time, so the place wasn't crowded, though a few people came in and out for snacks. Each time the door slid open, Peyton practically jumped out of her seat, but then the person would continue on to the snack bar without giving her a glance and she'd settle back down.

The allotted fifteen minutes passed and there was no sign of DF or Dryce. She pulled out her communicator to check and make sure that he hadn't canceled, but there was no message waiting for her.

Seventeen minutes passed. Then eighteen. And just before she was about to go crazy and send a message to DF demanding to know where he was Dryce walked through the door. His head swung around and he caught sight of her almost immediately. Their eyes locked and she saw it in his expression.

DF.

Dryce NaFeen.

Hers.

***

Dryce was braced for rejection. Especially given that he was a few minutes late due to an unexpected call from Sandon. He'd worried that Peyton had figured it out before he could explain, and he'd also worried that he'd walk in and she'd see him without realizing who he was.

But there was no risk of that. She recognized him, and if the heat in her eyes was anything to go by, she wasn't mad.

Well, not *completely* mad. He could see anger in the set of her shoulders and her jaw, but under it all was a simmering heat just waiting to explode.

Not here, though. This was far too public a place for this meeting.

Despite that, he slid into the seat across from her and sat silently, unsure of exactly what to say. He'd had grand ideas about revealing his identity, but now that the time had come, he knew that none of them would have worked. He'd lied to her and he had to own up to that now or they would never move forward.

And they *needed* to move forward. He needed her in his life and in his bed and at his side for the rest of his days. She was brilliant and beautiful and everything he'd never known he wanted. If she had just been some person he was trying to entice into his bed he would have known the right words, but he didn't know a magic phrase to convince her that he wanted more.

All he had was his honesty. And he could give her all of that.

"I'm sorry," he said before she could say anything else. "I should have told you who I was after we met."

Peyton let out an unsteady breath as her hands curled into fists where they rested on top of the table. "You should have told me the minute I mentioned you in our messages." It came out dangerously low through clenched teeth, as if she was afraid she'd yell if she spoke any louder.

Dryce nodded, but couldn't say it out loud. If he'd told her then, she would have cut off contact, and he'd cherished their conversations. "I—"

Peyton cut him off. "We shouldn't do this here."

They were both leaning close, each covering practically half of the small table until their faces were close enough to kiss. They were starting to get a few looks from interested occupants of the cafeteria and rumors were bound to be swirling about them already. Plenty of people talked about him, but Dryce didn't want Peyton to be the subject of gossip. It would be bad enough if she accepted their bond, and Dryce couldn't completely control what other people would say, but he could prevent this for now.

"I know a place," he said. He stood and without thinking offered his hand. He about jumped out of his skin when Peyton placed hers against his and linked their fingers together. They walked out of the cafeteria together as if the Earth hadn't just shifted beneath their feet and Dryce led her towards the temporary sleeping quarters where there were a variety of rooms available for on-call personnel.

He entered his ID on the wall panel to reserve the room and then he and Peyton were alone.

Tension thrummed in the air between them, but this was much different than anything that had bubbled up during the mission. For the first time they were together and Dryce was being completely honest. He was no longer split between two people, the typed messages of DF and the restrained conversation in person.

"Don't lie to me again," Peyton commanded. She glared at him, finger pointed and ready to attack if he made one wrong move.

Fire lived within her and even as Dryce didn't want to anger her, he drank in the sight. She glowed, absolutely awash in furious light. "I won't," he promised. It had been tearing him up inside to do it, every word he said another knot to bind him with. And now he was free, untied for the first time in weeks.

"Did you mean it?" She narrowed her eyes and pressed her lips together tightly as if to trap words in her mouth.

Dryce took a step forward until they were close enough to brush against one another. He wanted to touch, his fingers itched with the need, but he kept his hands to himself. She needed to make the first move if they were going to take this somewhere else. He hadn't brought her to this room for anything more than talk, but now that he realized they were in a private room with a bed right behind them, the promise of something more hung in the air. "Mean what?"

Peyton took several deep breaths, her shoulders lifting and falling with each one as if she'd just run a marathon. "All of it. Any of it."

It *hurt* not to reach out and touch her. "Every single word I've said."

She squeezed her eyes shut for a moment before opening them back up and piercing him with her gaze. "Why? Why me?"

This was the moment of truth. Once he said what he had to say, there was no turning back. "Because you're my denya."

Her mouth opened but no words followed. Her tongue darted out to lick her lips. "Your mate? Me?" She backed up a step and Dryce almost reached out, but he kept his hands at his sides as if they were shackled there. "So you just want me because there's no other choice. Fate told you that I… belonged to you or something?

I've read about the Denya Price. I know that you'll die if you don't mate with me."

"I noticed you because of the bond," Dryce conceded. He would have noticed her without it, but the recognition had bloomed so quickly that he hadn't had the chance. "But every moment I've spent with you, messaging you, talking to you, fighting with you," he grinned at that, even if it wasn't appropriate, "learning about you has made it clear that you're an amazing person. There is no one else I want but you, denya bond or not."

Chapter Fifteen

Dryce's words echoed through her mind, an impossible promise that she'd been dying to hear since she'd kissed him. Maybe even before that. He *wanted* her, he *belonged* to her. He was her mate. She couldn't believe it, and yet she could almost feel a connection thrumming between them, reaching out from her heart to his and binding them together through something that science couldn't hope to understand.

She could tell that he was holding himself back; tension vibrated off of his arms as if some invisible force were keeping him from reaching out for her. It would be easier if he did it, if he were to pull her close and crush their mouths and bodies together. Then she could say that she was caught up in the moment, that there'd never been a decision to make.

She wouldn't need to make a leap of faith.

Because he promised that he was looking for no other. But he'd lied before. Not about that, but about who he was to her, both by not telling her that he was DF and by omission when they'd discussed the denya bond. She should be mad about that, but Peyton couldn't bring herself back to that anger. It had fizzled out somewhere on their walk from the cafeteria and every defense she had was crumbling at the sheer heat in his eyes.

She'd wanted him from the first moment she'd seen him and now he said he was hers. What the hell was she waiting for?

She reached out and grabbed one of his hands, his skin hot under her fingertips. Dryce sucked in a breath as if the contact shocked him, and when she raised his hand to her cheek and brushed his fingers against her skin, his hand flexed. She let go, but he didn't lower his hand, and when his other hand cupped her hip she leaned into him.

"I'm your mate? Show me." She'd never considered using one of these on call rooms before, but she'd heard plenty of stories. Though a part of her worried about being caught, she wasn't about to delay this any longer by suggesting they head off the base. There was a perfectly functional bed less than a meter away and she had Dryce where she wanted him. Well, almost, but he'd be on top of her soon enough.

That was all the encouragement he needed before he took her mouth in a bruising kiss, conquering her with all the care of a man claiming a precious gift. Her fingers dug into the muscles of his sides and she arched against him, straining for contact. The taste of him was like a drug, heady and strong enough to make her dizzy, but she couldn't get enough. She didn't think she'd *ever* get enough.

When her spine met the hard wall she realized he'd backed her up and was crowding her until he became all that she knew in the world and she wouldn't have it any other way. She hooked her legs around his hips and felt the hard press of his cock through all of their layers of clothing. Too much clothing. Why did they wear it? It needed to come off *now*. But not if it meant giving up his mouth. She'd spent too many hours with the man *not* kissing him that now she needed to make up for lost time.

He devoured her like she was his last meal. And while he cherished her with every touch, he didn't treat her like she was made of glass. He might have been more than a head taller than her, nearly twice her size in muscle, and trained since a young age to fight, but he treated her like an equal.

If he kept doing it, Peyton was going to fall for him so hard she'd never recover.

And if he kept kissing her like this it wouldn't take long at all.

Her fingers quested for naked skin, tearing at his shirt and making a sound of frustration when her own legs kept it in place. It took a little doing, but she managed to expose the teal planes of his chest and finally get rid of the shirt, throwing it somewhere across the room. It still wasn't enough, not when she couldn't feel him against her own skin.

She struggled to get her top off and nearly fell over. Dryce smiled against her lips and urged her to lean back while he slowly unbuttoned her from neck to navel.

"Your eyes are red," she observed with heavy breaths. "I thought they were black." She'd spent enough time studying him while they were together that she could recall every detail with near perfect memory, but his eyes had never been like that before.

"It happens when a Detyen feels strong emotion," he said. "And there is nothing stronger than the denya bond."

That declaration sizzled through her and Peyton wanted more. She kissed him again, trusting him to hold all of her weight and pressing her torso to his, reveling in the feel of his naked flesh against hers. Her bra was still a frustration, but she didn't want to stop kissing to deal with it, not when Dryce showed her just how talented his tongue could be.

But as thrilling as it was to be pressed up against the wall and absolutely dominated by Dryce's control, the position had some drawbacks that made Peyton pull away and turn her head when Dryce tried to follow the kiss. He looked like a man possessed and she secretly thrilled at the fact that *she* had done this to him. He was mad with desire for *her*. No one had ever looked at her with such naked need and she could grow addicted to it.

A distant part of her warned that she should be cautious, that jumping into this could end in pain and heartache, but that part grew weaker by the minute as her lust mounted. The world could end any day, she wasn't going to throw this chance away just because she might get hurt.

She unwrapped herself from Dryce, even as her body yearned for the contact. *Soon you can have it all*, she promised herself, but she was greedy and she could practically feel a physical pull between them like they were two magnets reaching out for each other.

The light in the on call room was dim, barely enough to see by, and with Dryce's blue skin he seemed to blend into the shadows. She might have made it brighter if she knew where the lighting controls were, but instead she would just need to learn him by touch. She could drink him in with her eyes later.

"What do you want?" Dryce asked. His fingers skimmed over her shoulder and down until he found the clasps of her bra and freed her so they were both naked from the waist up. In other situations, she'd hated this part, being exposed to another person for their judgmental eyes.

But Dryce's eyes didn't judge, they *worshiped*. And the way he looked at her made all of her insecurities melt away. She was here with him, and that was all that mattered. For both of them. There was nothing but the present, nothing but the promise of right now, and realizing that was one of the most powerful things that Peyton had ever known.

She grazed her own hand across her stomach until she came to the clasp of her trousers. It didn't take much to shimmy them down, underwear and all, and end up naked in front of her man. He groaned and the twist deep in her core at that sound was only a promise of things to come. She stepped out of her fallen clothes and reached for him, but Dryce put a hand on her wrist.

"I don't want this to be over too soon." His voice came out low and gravelly, and the confession of how much he wanted her made her toes curl. Surely he had the control to hold back, but his eyes were still that deep ruby that only came while emotions ran high. "Lay down," he commanded, nodding towards the bed.

Peyton didn't like commands, didn't like giving up control. But when Dryce spoke like that, she wanted to surrender to him. And so she did. This thing between them was about pleasure, about joining together and confirming a bond she'd never thought possible. She didn't need to worry that he'd judge her for doing or saying the wrong thing. He wanted her just as desperately.

The bed wasn't wide, clearly made for a single person, and the mattress was practically hard as a rock. She didn't care. She was with Dryce and he was standing over her with the promise of everything in his red eyes. She could have been laying down on an actual rock and it still would have been perfect.

But it could be more perfect if the man at her feet actually joined her. She might not have been self-conscious, but the way he was looking at her made her want to squirm. "There's room enough for two," she promised.

Dryce grinned. "Is there really?"

Given that she was touching either side of the bed with her arms, he had a point. Not that she was going to let that stop him. "We can make it work."

"Spread your legs." He watched her with blatant ownership and Peyton loved it.

Her knee tipped to the side and she stretched her other leg out, baring herself completely to him. It was wicked and wanton and nothing she'd ever played at before, but with him she wanted it too much to be shy. And she was rewarded by the dark look that came over Dryce's face, promising her the kind of sensual prize she'd never known to reach for before.

He knelt on the edge of the bed and rubbed his cheek against the inside of her knee, trailing kisses up her thigh and then down the other, getting so close to the heart of her sex that she arched towards him, needing the touch. But he clearly had a plan, and that plan involved taking his time. Peyton wanted to whimper as her body cried out for more. Everywhere Dryce touched was a burning ember, but it wasn't enough, she wanted to be consumed by the flames of his desire.

His fingers found her first, playing in her wet heat and making her moan. It was barely a touch, but she was already so close to the edge that she was almost afraid for more. She'd never wanted something she feared so much in her life.

And then he added his lips and she was awash in sensation, writhing against the scratchy sheets of the bed and focused solely on what Dryce was doing to her. Her fingers curled into his soft hair and held him against her as helpless noises escaped her throat, inhuman and desperate and so nakedly honest that there was no hiding anything from the man beneath her.

Her breath caught and hitched and then Peyton cried out, chanting Dryce's name as the wave of her pleasure crested and her body rippled uncontrollably, hurtling her towards ecstasy all at the tips of Dryce's fingers and tongue.

But he wasn't done yet, and even as her mind was mush she didn't want it to be over. Not when he was hard and ready to enter her.

"Are you ready for me?" Dryce asked, his fingers preparing her for his entrance.

She didn't think she could string a sentence together, still delirious with satisfaction, but she managed a nod and a sound that might have been assent. It was enough. Dryce lined himself up at her entrance and the tip of his cock teased her. She wanted more. Needed more. Needed it *now*.

And then a sound cut through the near silence of the room, an annoying distraction from what Dryce was doing to her. "Ignore it," she urged. It had to be his communicator and whoever wanted to talk to him could wait.

But when a second alarm joined the first, they both cursed. That was her communicator. And the only reason they'd both be called was if something had come up with the mission.

Dryce pulled away from her and Peyton sat up, taking a long moment to survey his body. His cock was somewhat different than a human's, with enticing ridges she wanted to feel inside of her. She leaned forward to reach for him. If they couldn't finish this one way, at least she could give him this pleasure.

But their communicators chimed again and Dryce backed away, putting distance between them. "If you touch me now, denya, we will both end up ignoring our duties."

Peyton opened her mouth to argue. Then she remembered that the fate of the entire world rested on their shoulders and the lassitude that came with her orgasm was swept away as if it had never been there at all. She went to the washbasin beside the bed to quickly clean herself before putting her clothes back on.

"If the planet wasn't at risk of destruction I'd tell them to get back to us in an hour," she muttered.

Dryce chuckled and kissed the back of her neck. "An hour? I'd tell them to wait until morning."

Chapter Sixteen

Sandon eyed Dryce curiously when he walked into the room trailing behind Peyton. He wasn't one of the few members of the Detyen Legion who knew that Peyton was his mate, but that would be clear soon enough. Not now, though. Dryce would have gladly announced that Peyton wanted him to anyone who passed them by, but his mate was a private woman and wouldn't like it if he told the world what had just passed between them.

Of course his body was screaming at him to punch Sandon for interrupting them. Punch Sandon and then sling Peyton over his shoulder and take her back to their room and stay there until they were both satisfied.

"Is something wrong?" Sandon asked once they were seated. He looked at Dryce like he expected him to do something stupid. Did they really think he was reckless? Or was it the keyed up sexual tension he had to be exuding?

Peyton made a choked off sound, but Dryce spoke, hopefully before Sandon noticed it. "No problems here. I didn't expect to get called back tonight. I had plans."

"I'm sure whoever you left behind will get over the disappointment," Sandon replied dryly.

Dryce would have lunged forward if Peyton hadn't settled her hand on his thigh under the table, grounding him and keeping him in place. Her lips thinned at the reminder of Dryce's past, but she didn't pull away from him. "We're not here to talk about our personal lives, sir. What did you find?" Her voice came out cold, almost as flat as one of the soulless. She'd never spoken to him in that tone and Dryce hoped she never did.

Sandon pulled up several items on the holo player and let them play. A dozen Oscavians and Wreetans stood in the woods of the location Dryce and Peyton hadn't dared approach. In front of them was a massive piece of technology that reached almost to the treetops and was as wide around as a house. To the side of that was a teleporter landing port where a piece of equipment sat for a moment before the crew dragged it towards the machine. A moment later the landing port shimmered and another Wreetan appeared.

Dryce jolted in his seat. He'd seen that face before, though never in person. "That's Yormas of Wreet, isn't it?"

"We believe so," Sandon confirmed. "We can't be certain why he's chosen to come down to the planet, but we've put our forces on high alert, though it's likely he's already returned to his ship via the teleport. The analysts have raised the concern that he was doing a final inspection on his weapon and it could be armed at any moment. We've tasked a surveillance satellite to monitor the location, but the feeds we're getting back are unsatisfactory. They've done something to mask their activities from machine surveillance. The SDA wants to change strategy. They believe that Earth's defenses are more than a match for the fleet. Our only real concern has been the weapon. Sending a small team in to disarm it with all of those men there will guarantee they try to trigger it. Even if it only has a tenth of the power of the weapon that destroyed Detya, Earth might not survive."

"But if they're distracted, they might not realize that the weapon's location is compromised until it's too late," Dryce surmised.

"Correct." Sandon nodded. "We're making your team active and sending them in to cover Dr. Cho while she works on the mechanics. The SDA is prepping for an attack in the morning. We will need you in position to move in and do your part before dawn. If you're successful, this whole mess could be a memory by sundown. We'll be calling in your team shortly. Prepare to leave as soon as things are ready." He disabled the holo player and left the two of them sitting there alone.

Peyton squeezed his thigh before pulling away. She crossed her arms on the table and slumped forward. Dryce placed a hand on the small of her back and rubbed in gentle circles. "Are you alright?"

She huffed out a disbelieving laugh. "Alright? *Alright?* If I can't figure out how to disable a piece of alien tech that I've never seen before in the next few hours my entire planet, *billions* of people, are going to die. And everyone keeps looking at me like that's something I should just be able to deal with." She hid her head in her hands and Dryce thought he heard a sob.

His heart ached. He put his arms around her and when she leaned into him he gathered her close, pulling at her until she shifted out of her seat and sat in his lap, her arms going around his shoulders and her face fitting into the crook of his neck like it had been made to rest there. He could have sat like that for the rest of his life, if only his mate weren't crying, the pressure of the last few weeks finally catching up to her as she realized just how high the stakes of this mission actually were.

"This isn't something anyone is prepared for," he tried to reassure her. "No one should ever be asked to do what they need you to do." He kissed her cheek and tightened his hold. "But there's no one I trust more. You're the smartest person I've ever met. And if I can tell that after just a few weeks, the people who have worked with you for years have to be certain of it. They wouldn't have nominated you for the job if they didn't think you could do it."

"I don't know if I can," Peyton insisted, though her voice was more even now, more in control of her emotions. "If I had time to study it, to actually get my hands on the tech and *know* it inside and out, then yeah, sure, I could disarm a planet killing bomb. But with only, what, an hour? While we're under attack from a dozen hostile forces? That's not exactly an ideal working condition."

He smiled at her wry tone, and though some might assume that she needed calming words, he'd gotten to know his mate well enough that he wasn't about to give them. "Think of it this way. If you screw up, you won't have to worry about it for long."

She stilled and hiccupped before pulling back and giving his shoulder a light slap. "That's terrible!" But she was almost smiling. And she didn't seem to be falling apart anymore.

The door behind them opened and closed just as quickly.

Peyton looked up and her cheeks took on a deliciously red tone. She gave his lips a quick peck before sliding off of his lap and back into her own chair. Dryce immediately missed the connection and reached out, linking their hands together.

"We can do this," he assured her. And he hoped with all that lived within him that he was right.

***

Quinn stretched out against Kayde, her body almost sated enough to knock her into oblivion. Who would have thought having a massive alien warrior share her bed every night would be such a good thing? Everyone who'd tried it, that was who. And the last few nights without him while he was out on his mission had screwed her up. She'd gotten used to sleeping the whole night through in their bed with him beside her. With him gone it had been like her life before they realized they were mates and she'd barely snatched more than an hour or two.

She curled up against him and rested her hand on his naked chest. Kayde's hand covered hers and he kissed her cheek. "I do not like sleeping without you, denya," he murmured, clearly holding onto consciousness by sheer force of will. They got like this sometimes, neither one of them wanting to surrender their moments together to the darkness of sleep. Eventually one of them would fall into unconsciousness and the other would follow soon behind. But not quite yet.

"I hate it," Quinn replied. She moved her leg over his, tracing her toe over his calf and watching Kayde shiver at the sensation. If she kept doing it, giving these playful touches, she knew he'd rise to the occasion and they'd put off sleep for a little longer, and there was no harm in that. She loved touching him, loved the simple intimacy that came from being near him. She'd never known a relationship could be like this and wouldn't have believed someone if they told her. Now she didn't want to let go of her mate, not even for a minute. "I'm meeting with the survivors tomorrow," she informed him. They hadn't spent much time talking when he'd come through the door. She'd kind of jumped him and torn his clothes off. The mating bond was still new and strong between them, and looking at Kayde, no one could blame her. He was the sexiest being on the planet.

"That's good," Kayde replied. "Has there been any progress on integrating Laurel into the group?"

Quinn groaned and hid her head against his chest. "Laurel is reluctant, not that I blame her, and a few of the women are outright hostile. Even after knowing for certain that she had a chip in her head controlling her actions. Maybe it's guilt for what some of them did." Leaving a woman to die in the midst of battle might do that to some people. Quinn wasn't certain who among her fellow survivors had abandoned Laurel, and she doubted it was a mystery that would ever be solved. "We'll talk about it some more, but they're more worried about the rumors that the planet is under attack." Rumors she knew were closer to being true than false.

"And what do you plan to tell them?" Kayde played with her hair, running his fingers over it and letting it wrap around his fingers.

"Some version of the truth. They won't go to the press. Besides, Muir is likely to know more than the average person if her uncle is feeding her info. No specifics though." Not that Quinn had many specifics of her own to give, but she wouldn't tell her friends any information that could get her mate hurt. She trusted those women... mostly. But she'd also seen how they acted under pressure, and she wasn't about to put the fate of the planet in their hands.

"When this is over we should go away someplace, just the two of us," Kayde suggested. "I want you to show me the wonders of our home."

Hearing Kayde's certainty that they'd make it through the coming weeks and the violence that was certain to come did a lot to help settled Quinn's nerves. She was doing her damnedest not to show them. She was mated to an alien warrior and with that came a cost. He had to fight for his people, had to fight to defend his new home. She couldn't ask him to sit the battle out, to hide away in safety. Especially not *this* battle. Safety was only an illusion when the army at their doorstep might have a weapon that could destroy the planet with the press of a button.

"I'd like that. How does the beach sound?" She'd never traveled before, not except for the accidental adventure that had landed her a mate. And while there'd been a certain beauty to the icy outpost the Detyens had once called home, she much preferred a place where she could relax in a bathing suit with plenty of tasty drinks available whenever she wanted.

"I—" The shrill ring of Kayde's communicator cut him off and he was out of bed like a shot, all traces of drowsiness gone between one blink and the next. He reached for the device and answered the call, his voice clipped with whoever he was talking to. After a moment he disconnected and set his comm back down, shooting a regretful look back at Quinn.

"You have to go back in," she surmised. They'd known that this reprieve wouldn't last long, though she'd expected to at least have until morning.

"There's been a development," Kayde confirmed.

She could argue. She could rant about their stolen hours and complain that life wasn't fair. But that wouldn't stop Kayde from going in, it would only make them both feel worse about it. So she sat up and kissed him slowly, pouring every milliliter of her love into it. When she pulled back, her mate's eyes had gone red and she knew it wouldn't take much to have him back inside her. So she kept enough distance to make sure that didn't happen, not when he had a duty. "Come back to me," she commanded.

"Always, denya."

Chapter Seventeen

They were in a heli-jet this time, much bigger than the helicopter that Peyton and Dryce had used to travel between locations before. With a team of seven and a pilot who'd been introduced as Jo, they needed the extra space. Peyton's nerves were on edge. After the meeting, she'd managed to snatch a few hours of sleep, but it had been fitful, full of nightmares where she couldn't save the planet and everyone died.

Maybe it would have been better if she could have slept beside Dryce, but they'd both known that if they went back into an on call room together they wouldn't do anything approaching rest. Though maybe she'd be a little less stressed out.

She was sitting next to him now, her mind reeling at how much things could change in a day. He was her *mate*? He was *hers?* How had that happened? It had all seemed so marvelous when they were making out, it had all made sense, but when she snatched glances of the beautiful alien beside her she almost couldn't reconcile the fact that he wanted her, that he said they were made for one another.

Ella was going to freak out.

That was the first thought that made her smile all morning. Her sister was such an alien groupie that she'd see it as one of the great injustices of the universe that Peyton had managed to fall in love with the sexiest alien of them all.

In love? Oh, um. She tried to keep her expression neutral as the thought ricocheted around her mind. Was she really in love with him? So soon? Was that even possible? Sure, he'd said they were mates or whatever, but that was physical, biological. Emotions grew from it, but she barely knew the guy.

Except that wasn't exactly true. She'd spent the last weeks getting to know him over the comms, and the last few days by his side night and day. She'd seen the dedicated warrior that lived behind the playboy façade, knew that he was so much more than anyone thought of him. Knew he cared for her deeply and wanted her even more.

"It's going to be alright," Dryce murmured against her ear, his hand landing gently on her thigh. None of the Detyens or the human, Sierra, spared them a glance.

Peyton didn't know if it was because they knew about her connection to Dryce or if they just expected him to act that way. She kind of hoped it was the first. She was getting used to the fact that he was hers, and she didn't want anyone to think that Dryce was going out there and flirting with anything that moved. Well, he could flirt, he had a naturally flirtatious air and she wasn't about to change his good humor, but it ended at *that* and when it came to the touching and the kissing and everything else, he belonged to her.

She swallowed against the huge lump of strong emotions and took a moment to make sure her tone came out even. "I'm fine," she said. The relationship anxiety was almost a blessing. She'd much rather worry about that then the fact that if she failed in the next few hours she was dooming Earth to destruction.

Fuck. There was that other anxiety. Her hands shook, but she curled them into fists and kept them in her lap, fiercely denying any urge to fidget.

Toran, the gold alien who seemed to be the team leader, sat forward in his seat after they'd been in the air for about fifteen minutes. The seven seats they were sitting in all faced the central corridor of the jet, so none of them had to turn around or shift to see him. He pulled out a mini-holo player and brought up the surveillance footage they'd captured earlier.

"When we receive the signal, Team One will advance to engage with the hostiles on the ground while Team Two will wait for the second signal. Once they've got that, they'll advance to the device and Dr. Cho will do what she's here to do. Everyone stay on high alert. There are no second chances on this mission." His face was a mask of surety. He'd worked with these people before and knew how they functioned as a team. He was a pure warrior, had fought many times before and survived victorious. Peyton wished she had a little of his confidence, but she'd have to take the heat of Dryce beside her and all his faith and use that to fool herself into believing that she wasn't afraid.

Toran went over a few more things, and at the end invited any questions, but the team had none. They traveled the rest of the way with everyone making companionable conversation as if they might not die in the next hour. Peyton didn't know how they did it. She was made for the lab, not battle.

The jet set down several kilometers away from their destination and the team prepped their gear before taking off on their hike, leaving Jo to guard the jet and wait as backup in case she was called. While an aerial attack could end the coming fight before it began, they couldn't risk damaging the waiting bomb and accidentally triggering it.

The weight of the improvised kill switch seemed to drag down Peyton's entire pack. She wouldn't be happy until she could tear the guts out of the planet killing machine and assure herself that it would never see the light of day again. Even knowing just how much powerful tech could be contained in a small device, she wasn't comfortable. Not when the stakes were this high. Not when the planet was at stake.

By now the SDA had to be preparing for takeoff. The sun was just creeping up over the horizon and it would be daylight before long. That didn't mean much for a battle destined to happen at the end of the solar system, but it was their cue to begin their journey towards their destination where they'd wait under cover for the next signal.

They walked in near silence and Peyton was incredibly aware that she was the person making the most noise. Dryce and his people must have trained to move through rough terrain on stealthy feet, and Sierra as well. Peyton wished that she could just say it was some special Detyen trait, but the human woman proved her wrong.

Damnit, she was a doctor, not a soldier.

Time shifted around them, one minute blending into the next until Peyton was shocked to see it was full light, the bright beams of sun breaking through the canopy overhead. It would be sweltering if they weren't in the shade, especially given all of the gear they were carrying, so she was happy for the protections. She just wanted this to be done.

Toran gave a hand signal and they all came to a halt. A sense of anticipation lit the air around them. They had to be close, just out of range of any standard surveillance protocols that the Oscavians or Wreetans may have been using. And now they waited.

And waited.

The sun climbed even higher overhead and sweat tickled the back of Peyton's neck. She wished she had something to keep her entertained, a game on her communicator, a particularly tricky piece of tech to figure out, or even just conversation with one of her companions, but they needed to remain silent and ready. They could get their signal at any moment, and even if they didn't, they needed to be prepared in case the enemy spotted them.

She hated the tension, the waiting, she just wanted this to be done, no matter how terrifying the prospect of her responsibility was.

She glanced at Dryce and their eyes met. He offered a small smile and though it shouldn't have done much, it steadied her, reminded her that she wasn't alone in this. She still had a lot to talk about with that man, *everything* to figure out. What did it mean to be mated? Where did their relationship go? Were they dating? Did he love her? Did he wish he hadn't met her?

Okay, maybe she wouldn't ask all of that. She didn't need him to know just how insecure she was when it came to him, not on top of her insecurity about saving the planet.

Ha! If she rewound the clock a month and told her past self what was about to happen, that Peyton would have laughed in her face.

Dryce grabbed her hand and placed a kiss on her knuckles, crashing through all her doubts and landing his place securely in her heart. Yeah, they needed to talk, but if he kept looking at her like that talking would be the last thing on her mind when she got him alone.

And out of danger.

Even knowing this was his job, she really wished that he could stay out of the line of fire.

Around her the soldiers came to attention even though she hadn't heard or seen anything.

Then Toran made a gesture and it all became clear.

The signal had come in. It was time to move.

***

As the rest of the team moved on, Dryce waited for the second signal. He and Peyton couldn't move forward until most of the hostiles were pulled away from the weapon. It would be no use to charge in quickly and be cut down by blaster fire before they had a chance to do what they were there to do.

Peyton's eyes were closed and her bottom lip trembled. Her honey skin had gone a bit pale and she looked like one harsh wind would shatter her into pieces. He wished he could remove her from this danger, that this responsibility didn't lay heavy on her shoulders. But she was their best hope for survival.

And she hadn't fallen apart yet. Yes, she'd wished this was someone else's responsibility, and she feared that she wouldn't live up to the task. But she was here now and still standing, and only the strongest of people could do that despite their fears.

He believed in her with his entire being, and not only because she was his mate. Their bond was a blessing, but her intelligence was all her own and it was an honor to watch her work. Or it would be. And Dryce would do everything he could to see her safely through it.

A red light flashed on his watch, their sign to move.

He waved Peyton forward and she followed close behind him. She didn't carry a weapon, having never been trained with anything that might be useful. That didn't matter. If Toran and the rest of the team were doing their job, his blaster would be more than sufficient to see this through.

Yormas's weapon was the size of a building and as Dryce and Peyton cleared the tree line it became apparent that it actually *was* a building. Two Wreetans ran out of an entrance, both carrying las rifles and heading towards where trouble brewed.

Dryce pulled out a scanner and pointed it at the weapon, calibrating it for living beings. Whatever the weapon was made of messed with his signal. The scan returned an inconclusive result. Dryce tilted the screen towards Peyton so she could read it and heard her hiss out a breath. He wanted to look back and reassure her, but he had to keep his eyes open for the enemy.

They waited another minute, but no one else came running out of the building. "If anyone is in there, they're likely to stay put," Dryce murmured. "But the main forces are engaged now."

Peyton let out a breath. "Then let's get this done."

They moved forward cautiously, Dryce's scanner active but still only offering inconclusive results. It started blinking and protesting the closer they got to the weapon and when they were only a few meters from the entrance Dryce turned it off. If it wasn't going to work, he didn't need the distraction.

Unlike the warehouse from the day before, there was no forcefield to keep them from entering.

He led Peyton inside, his blaster drawn and senses on high alert. Sound echoed all around them, a symptom of the metal walls that towered overhead. The entire thing was made of metal, with a catwalk along the ceiling to access several hubs, and every few meters there were recesses in the walls. Dryce couldn't tell what anything was for, but he never would have guessed this place was a weapon. It looked more like a space ship than anything else.

"This place kind of looks like my first apartment," Peyton admitted. Her voice carried with the strange acoustics and Dryce tensed, but no one came after them for the sound.

He hoped that meant they were alone, but he didn't dare believe it. "What are we looking for?" There was no convenient red button that said "SHUT DOWN WEAPON OF MASS DESTRUCTION" and he hoped Peyton had better ideas.

She pulled a small device out of her pocket and it took Dryce a moment to realize it was the piece of tech that had been recovered from Brakley Varrow's belongings. "I need to hook this up somewhere. Once we're connected I can get to work. Look for a junction box, or some place with exposed wiring."

He was too busy looking for the enemy to do that, but he kept alert while Peyton looked. There was nothing on the ground floor, but when his denya tilted her head up towards the catwalk her eyes narrowed. Thin shafts of sunlight came in through openings above their heads and one seemed to illuminate one of the hubs up there.

She pointed. "That looks like a good bet."

Dryce didn't like it. They'd make a lot of noise climbing one of the ladders and they'd be exposed while he needed at least one hand to haul himself up. "You're sure there's nothing down here?"

"Not that I've seen." Peyton took another look around, but she was already shaking her head before she'd finished her scan. "If anyone can just waltz in like this, it would make sense not to keep the important stuff on the ground, right? Not to mention the risk of weather or wild animals."

On that he had to agree. So Dryce led her to the nearest ladder and let her climb first. They hadn't seen anyone on the catwalk which was completely exposed. The bigger danger came from someone below.

Peyton climbed quickly, but not quietly. She clambered up and Dryce gave her a minute before heading up behind her, keeping one hand on his blaster just in case someone showed up. It meant that he couldn't go as fast as he would have liked, but they weren't completely vulnerable to a threat.

And it was the right move. He'd only moved up three rungs when a shout rang out. Without saying anything, Peyton scrambled up faster, abandoning any pretense of stealth. Dryce swung around and started firing, wincing as a blast hit the wall of the weapon and set wires sizzling. He took his finger off the trigger, quickly realizing that he could set this thing off if he wasn't careful.

Above him Peyton grunted, but he couldn't spare her a glance when he saw a figure covered in body armor coming out of what he'd thought was just another recess in the wall. Dryce aimed his blaster and shot, even knowing it was no match for the armor. And he was right. All it did was tell the hostile where he and Peyton were.

Rather than defend his position on the ladder he jumped off the three rungs and rolled, coming up right at the feet of the armor clad soldier. Hand to hand combat was almost pointless. But body armor could withstand fists, not claws. He kept shooting his blaster, more as a distraction than with any hope of making contact, while the claws of his left hand slid out, wickedly long and sharp, a throwback to a time before Detyens had been civilized.

He dug those claws in against the joint of the armor and grinned when something shorted in the mechanics. The hostile let out a grunt and aimed a punch to Dryce's jaw, but with him so close the angle was off and it glanced off his shoulder. Fire radiated down the limb and he dropped the blaster and his claws were nearly wrenched out of the hostile's armor. But Dryce held on. If he didn't fell the enemy, Peyton was defenseless. He couldn't let that happen. He would not fail his mate.

No longer worrying about his blaster, he swiped at the armor with his right hand as well, digging in around the neck and looking for weak points. He was all wrapped around the soldier and while it meant he took blows that battered his ribs and were sure to leave his skin bruised and sickly, the soldier didn't have enough leverage to do real damage.

And there was nothing that could make Dryce let go.

Finally, a clasp of the helmet released with a hiss and Dryce managed to sneak his claws in, digging into soft flesh and making blood spurt.

And now the soldier took him seriously. He bucked and managed to throw Dryce off, kicking him until something cracked and Dryce could taste the metallic hint of blood in his mouth. It didn't matter. He had to get this done.

He threw himself back at the soldier, doing his best to break through the armor that was already coming off in patches. And the man under the armor was fading fast, his blood pouring out of the wound that Dryce had managed to make. It might not have been fatal if the man had time to get to a medic. But with his heart pumping blood out every second, the man didn't have much longer.

His next punch was too light to do any damage, and when Dryce backed up two steps the soldier tried to follow. But he stumbled. And then fell. Blood pooled around him, but Dryce waited. He wasn't going to turn his back until he was sure the enemy was dead.

And once that was done, he wasted no time climbing up the ladder and joining Peyton, keeping enough distance so she wouldn't be sickened by all the blood.

She looked over at him and her face held such defeat the he looked for the wound, but she was completely unharmed. Her hand rested on the device she'd brought from the lab and her head was bowed. "It's not working," she lamented. "There's nothing I can do."

Chapter Eighteen

Peyton couldn't pay any attention to what Dryce was doing on the ground floor. It was her time to shine. But when she found her way into the system, it quickly became clear that anything she'd hoped to accomplish wouldn't be happening. All of her research counted on the device using Wreetan, Oscavian, or Earth technology, and the only reason she'd thrown Earth into the mix was because it was her home. She'd been almost certain it would depend on Wreetan engineering, since that was where Yormas was from.

What she was looking at now was like nothing she'd ever seen before. She did a scan, but whatever was in the walls was messing with her equipment. Her only hope was that the trigger she'd turned into a kill switch might do thc job.

But when she pressed the button nothing happened.

Dryce clambered up the ladder, covered in blood and looking like he'd just crawled home from battle. But there was still hope in his eyes, a hope that Peyton couldn't let grow. She waved the kill switch at him as her shoulders sagged. "It's not working. There's nothing I can do."

Dryce opened his mouth as if to offer words of encouragement, but quickly snapped it shut. He knew what she was capable of, and he had to know that if she said it couldn't be done, then it couldn't.

But there *had* to be another way. They hadn't come this far just to know the planet was doomed. Even if all Peyton could do was kill whatever trigger mechanisms there were so Yormas was forced to come down to the planet again and trigger the damn thing himself, that would be better than nothing.

She stood, taking a deep breath and glancing out the opening near the roof. A green scent of the wood outside filtered in, momentarily blocking out all the metal around her. But it wasn't the trees that caught her attention. She could just make out a corner of the teleportation pad from where she was standing, but it was enough and a light went off in her mind.

"That could work," she muttered. "Maybe." Teleporters were tricky beasts and prone to failure when not calibrated correctly and constantly monitored. But Peyton just wanted the thing off her planet. She didn't care where the bomb went after that.

Well, that wasn't quite true. She didn't want to doom another civilization by sending it to the wrong place, but if the teleporter was already programmed to send things to somewhere in Yormas's fleet, she couldn't feel too bad about returning their weapon to them and letting it wreak its havoc.

"What are you thinking?" Dryce asked. She must have been quiet for some time as she went over the variables.

It wasn't difficult to reprogram a teleporter, and from the look of the landing base she was willing to bet that Yormas was using a type that was mass produced in the Oscavian Empire. Peyton had seen plenty of those.

She could do this.

"We need to get out there." She nodded out the window.

Dryce came to stand at her side and looked out, trying to see what she'd seen. "Back in the forest? Why?"

"Not the forest. I can't disable this bomb, so I'm going to make it go away."

They didn't waste any time talking after that. Dryce led them back down the ladder but there were no hostile forces to meet them. The forest seemed quiet around them and Peyton hoped that was because the Detyen team had been successful in their mission.

Once they were close to the teleporter she pulled out her gear and fashioned a connection, smashing through the basic security with ease. She preferred to deal with physical products rather than hacking through code, but she had skills enough to change some basic coordinates to get this done. The Oscavians knew how to make a user friendly device and she would have been grateful to them if there weren't a bunch of them intent on destroying the planet.

The sound of footsteps cut through her concentration and she looked over to see the Detyen team making their way back. They were covered in dirt and one of Dru's arms seemed to be hanging unnaturally, but they were all accounted for.

"The hostiles?" Dryce asked, scanning behind them to make sure no one else was coming.

"Taken care of," Toran confirmed. "What's the status?"

Peyton sat back on her heels and rolled her neck from one side to the other, trying to work out the kinks. "I can't disable it. I don't recognize the engineering, it's too alien. I'm reprogramming the teleporter. If all goes as planned, we'll be sending this little chunk of forest out into space where Yormas can deal with it."

"And that will work?" Kayde asked. "Could he just send it back?"

"Maybe," Peyton conceded. She was too much of a scientist to rule out the possibility just to offer comfort to her team. "But it will likely be damaged, possibly beyond repair, and if it gets exposed to the vacuum and radiation of space, it could further disrupt whatever makes it function. Either way, it won't be a direct threat to Earth anymore. At worst I'm buying some time." And she hoped it was more than that, hoped that this would be enough to quell the alien threat. She wanted her planet and her people to be safe, and she didn't want a weapon like this to exist anymore. No one needed this much destructive power.

"I'll trust your judgment," said Toran.

"Then I need all of you to get back. You need to be at least a kilometer away from this thing when I trigger the teleporter. I should have it configured correctly, it *should* just take the weapon, but since it's no longer directly working off the teleportation pad, something could go wrong." If Peyton had a few hours, or preferably days, to get things right, she'd know the exact coordinates that would be sent. But even with an easy Oscavian system, she was still putting it together mostly with ingenuity and hope.

The request didn't seem to faze Toran. "Very well. Let's head out." But they didn't move immediately and Peyton realized they were waiting for her.

"I'll need to stay here," she said. "I should be safe, but I can't do this remotely." She could risk herself, risk being transported into the black of space or onto an enemy ship, but she wasn't going to risk the team.

"I'm staying with you," Dryce said before anyone could object to her announcement.

She'd expected it. Peyton didn't want to put her mate in danger, but a part of her was grateful to have him at her side. If he was here, nothing could go wrong, right? "Dryce stays," she agreed. "But the rest of you need to go. Please." She wasn't in charge, she knew Toran or any of the others could countermand her declaration, but she was willing to beg. There was no use risking them all.

Toran gave Dryce a hard stare before returning his gaze to her and giving a single nod. "Give us a few minutes to clear the distance. We'll expect you at the ship when this is done."

"We'll be there," Dryce promised.

Peyton hoped she could make him keep his word.

The team left, leaving her and Dryce alone with the teleportation pad. Peyton went over the settings three times, and then a fourth and fifth for good measure. She'd relied on a mapping application on her communicator to grab the coordinates of the weapon. It wasn't exact, but she wasn't too concerned about cutting off bits and pieces if that ended up happening. Whatever destruction it could do once it was strewn in pieces across land and space was nothing compared to what it would do if she just left it sitting there.

And now there was nothing to do but send it away.

The team had been given plenty of time to make their retreat. Peyton counted down another minute in her head just in case. Then she looked over at Dryce and offered an over confident smile. "Ready for this?"

He nodded and placed his hand on her shoulder in a show of support.

Peyton pressed the launch button and sent up a prayer to anyone that was listening.

A beat pulsed through the forest, and she could feel it deep inside her. Her ears popped, and the air in front of her shimmered before the weapon slowly dissolved right before her eyes. She almost couldn't believe it. It took several minutes to disappear completely, a testament to the device's complexity, and when the teleportation was done a giant crater filled the forest where the weapon used to sit.

Peyton turned around and threw her arms around Dryce as relief surged through her. She'd done it! *They'd* done it. The planet was safe. At least from this threat.

But before Peyton could say anything, something coiled around her throat and she was tugged back, and before she could realize what was happening, everything went black.

Chapter Nineteen

The screeching of metal and an otherwise eerie silence woke Peyton from her little nap. Her eyes flew open, and as she snapped immediately to consciousness she realized she hadn't been asleep at all. No, she'd blipped out while teleporting right alongside the giant bomb she'd banished from the planet.

And now that bomb was straining the bounds of whatever room she was in, tearing at the sturdy metal and sending a support beam crashing to the floor. The room was gargantuan, and at one point there must have been a teleportation hub in the middle of it all, but her little trick had seen that destroyed with the press of a button. She was just lucky that she wasn't under all those tons of metal.

She nearly jumped out of her skin when she felt a hand on her shoulder, but a moment later she realized it was Dryce materializing beside her and relief rushed through her. She didn't want to be alone out here. They had to be in space. Gravity didn't feel exactly right, too heavy, like the system wasn't calibrated correctly, or maybe it was simply what these soldiers were used to back on their planet.

"That can't be good," Dryce said, pointing to where half of the bomb was disappearing into one of the ship's walls.

"We're lucky that it's on the interior. If the hull had been breached…" Peyton shuddered to think of the results. "But someone's going to come check this out soon." They needed to get back to Earth, not only because it was home, but because she didn't trust this ship to stay intact for long. If the weapon had caused severe structural damage, which it seemed was the case, they didn't have much time. Not to mention the Earth forces attacking the Oscavian and Wreetan fleet.

"We can find an escape pod," Dryce suggested. "That will get us out of here quick enough."

Peyton glanced around, taking in the damage to their surroundings. She didn't see a door, but from the way the weapon was blocking everything, she'd bet there was one hidden along one of the walls. "I was thinking of something a bit—aha!" Her eyes locked on the control console, which seemed to be intact. "As long as our teleport here didn't damage the system too much, we can be home in no time." Normally Peyton wouldn't trust a compromised teleporter, but she didn't want to risk going further into the ship. The teleport had already proved it could transport her and Dryce safely once, she was willing to chance it again.

"Even without that hub?" Dryce asked. He, too, was looking around, though he seemed more focused on looking for threats.

"We'll see. Now help me." Peyton rushed over to the console without waiting for Dryce to catch up. But he was right behind her and together they cleared a little bit of fallen debris and she looked over the display to see what her first step needed to be.

Somewhere hidden by a huge chunk of a metal something groaned too loud to be anything living. At least she hoped it wasn't. Only something like a giant could make a sound that loud and resonant, and they *really* couldn't deal with a giant right now. Peyton's tongue darted out to lick her lips. "You do have your blaster, right?"

Dryce patted the holster in confirmation. "I'm going to search the perimeter for any danger. If it gets dangerous, take cover."

She bit back a sarcastic reply, but before Dryce could move away she reached out and grabbed his hand, tugging him close for a swift kiss. "Be careful. Come back to me."

"Always, denya." His eyes briefly flashed red and he gave her a kiss of his own before backing away.

Peyton watched him go until he disappeared before some of the fallen metal, and then she forced herself to get to work. They both had jobs to do. Dryce had to keep her safe, to keep them both safe, and she had to find a way to swiftly get them home. She'd already screwed up once by accidentally transporting them to this ship. She couldn't screw up again.

Just like the teleportation pad on Earth, the device on the ship was of Oscavian make. As she pulled up the information screens she was relieved to see that everything seemed to be functioning as well as could be expected with a giant, planet-killing bomb landing on top of the machine. Hell, it was functioning much better than could be expected. But Peyton quickly realized they had a problem.

The weapon had landed in the heart of the teleportation hub, and she couldn't pull the same trick that she'd managed back on Earth. That piece of creative programming had counted on the fact that they had a stable hub waiting for them, one that had already been programmed into the teleporter. With no landing pad on the other end and no hub to power the whole thing now, she had to start from square one and figure out a new way home.

But she had a teleporter, she could do this.

She smelled the thick ozone in the air half a second before she heard the shot of a blaster. Her head snapped up and she saw Dryce retreating, taking cover behind any standing metal he could find as he fired wildly back at whoever was shooting at him.

Peyton winced and spared a glance at the weapon she'd brought back with them. She hoped the shots weren't enough to set it off, but still she worried. Though, she reasoned, if it was stable enough to survive a teleport without exploding, a few hits of blaster fire probably wouldn't hurt it.

She put that out of her mind and did her best to focus on the problem in front of her. Get them home. Nothing else mattered.

***

Dryce wanted to yell at Peyton to hurry up. The blaster shots were coming in faster and faster by the moment, and he was sure that a contingent of Oscavian and Wreetan soldiers were going to charge through the opening to the rest of the ship that he'd found at any moment. It wasn't a door; instead a large gash had been torn in one of the walls. Distantly he heard a siren wailing and he was almost certain that evacuation procedures were being carried out.

The few soldiers he'd actually seen were wearing full on survival suits, so even if the life support on the ship gave out, they'd have enough time to make it to an escape pod or would survive in empty space long enough for a rescue.

He and Peyton didn't have that advantage, and as he was looking at the only exit out of the teleportation chamber, he had to hope that Peyton figured out a way to get them back to Earth quickly. It would take his blaster a long time to overheat, but it wasn't much of a match against survival suit clad soldiers.

He risked a glance back at his mate and saw her hunched over the console, her face screwed up in concentration. It almost seemed like she didn't realize they were under fire, but she flinched as a barrage of fire from the enemy went wide and echoed in the cavernous chamber.

He needed to protect her. He needed to buy her time.

The sirens suddenly got louder and the shots stopped. Dryce breathed heavily and didn't dare move. He heard marching steps and couldn't believe his ears as they grew fainter and fainter. Were they really retreating?

"How's it going over there?" he called to Peyton.

She actually growled and then slapped her hand against the edge of the console. "Not well. You'd be surprised how delicate these things are."

Dryce didn't know how to respond to that and Peyton didn't seem to expect a reply. She absently ran her fingers through her hair before ducking out of sight, presumably to get a look at some of the wiring under the console.

Dryce strained to hear anything coming from the hallway, but the siren drowned most other sounds out. He risked darting a glance around the corner and didn't see anyone lying in wait. Rather than risk it he picked up a piece of debris and tossed it into the corridor to see if anyone would flinch or shoot.

No sounds. No shots.

With not much other choice, Dryce went low and ducked into the opening, breaking for cover closer to the hallway. His heart beat hard enough to pound out of his chest, but no one shot, and the closer he got to the opening in the wall the more certain he became that the enemy had retreated.

For some reason.

He didn't like it.

He made it to the opening in the wall and glanced out. There was no one to be seen. The wailing of the siren got even more shrill, pulsing an insistent beat, and in the distance he could just make out an announcement filtering in through a speaker somewhere. His translator made easy work of the Oscavian, and as he heard the words ice lanced his heart.

"Self-destruct sequence activated. Evacuate immediately. Fifteen minutes until detonation."

That explained the retreat. There was no need to shoot him or Peyton when the entire ship was about to blow up. He turned and ran back to his mate and hoped she had good news for him. But she was still hunkered under the console and swearing quietly when he made it back.

"How much more time is this going to take?" He tried to keep the urgency out of his voice, tried not to make it seem like they were in a rush, but he couldn't conceal it all.

Peyton shimmied back into the open. "It will take as long as it takes," she groused. "Do you want to try rewiring it?"

She seemed ready to come to blows and the pressure mounted on top of pressure that she'd been through over the last few days was surely catching up. But they didn't have time to argue. "The ship's about to blow." Dryce kept his tone matter of fact. There was no use for panic, that was a sure way to end up dead quick. "We have fifteen minutes. Can you fix the teleporter in that time?"

Her eyes widened before growing wet with worry. "I—maybe? What if the answer is no?" She glanced back at the console, her eyes darting madly from one indicator to the next.

"Then we find another way off this ship." Dryce reached out and rested his hand on his mate's. "You saved the planet. You did amazing. It's alright if we can't use the teleporter again. But we need to hurry."

She dragged in a shaky breath and cast her gaze back at him. "Fifteen minutes isn't enough time."

Dryce nodded once. "Then we're going. Follow me."

They skirted around some debris to make it to the makeshift door. The sound of the blaring siren distorted everything around them and though Dryce strained to hear if anyone was coming towards them. He couldn't hear anything except the horn and the warning that time was running short. His senses were on high alert, ready to meet any threat, but they didn't have time for any long, drawn out fight. Their only advantage at the moment was that any soldier they met would be in the same situation.

And things wouldn't exactly improve if they found an escape pod. They were ejecting into the midst of an enemy fleet and that fleet was under bombardment from Earth forces who'd have no way of knowing that Dryce and Peyton were in one of the escape vessels.

They'd need to worry about that later.

But they hadn't seen anyone before they came to the first escape vessel. It became obvious why when the indicator beside the escape pod door showed that the vehicle had already jettisoned. They said nothing, just continued to move further into the ship.

There was little sign of the damage that they'd escaped in the teleportation room. If Dryce hadn't seen it himself, he would have wondered why the ship had engaged its self-destruct sequence.

The second escape vessel station they found had also been jettisoned and Dryce's worry grew as the countdown warned them that they had less than ten minutes to escape. The found a station stocked with survival suits and paused to put them on. It wouldn't do much good if the ship imploded around them, but neither he nor Peyton mentioned that. His mate had a look of grim determination on her face and he was sure that she was thinking of all the alternatives for survival if they didn't find an escape pod.

They almost walked into a cluster of Oscavian soldiers, and it was only the clatter of something hitting the ground that warned Dryce to stop before they rounded a corner and gave themselves away. The survival suits might have bought them a second or two, but they weren't much in the way of a disguise.

His arm shot out to bar Peyton from moving any further forward and Dryce crept as close as he dared, trying to get a look. He watched as an Oscavian darted into an escape vessel and pulled the door shut behind him. Footsteps pounded down the hallway and a desperate cry sounded as someone begged them to wait, but even down the hallway Dryce could hear the vessel taking off.

The abandoned soldier cursed and slammed something against the wall. Dryce eased back until he was beside Peyton. He readied his blaster in case the soldier came their way, but he didn't want to engage if he could avoid it. There was no telling how many soldiers were left aboard and he didn't want to waste time with a fight. And given the soldier's reaction to losing out on a seat on that escape vessel, lifeboats were becoming more scarce by the minute.

They waited for several long seconds, but the Oscavian gave a final curse and must have turned away, his footsteps fading in the direction that he'd come.

Peyton and Dryce continued on, but they'd only made it a little ways before Peyton patted his arm to make him stop.

Seven minutes left.

She nodded towards a door with a symbol on it that he didn't recognize. "Shipping room," she whispered. "There could be an intact teleporter in there, or there could be a short range ship. I've studied enough Oscavian schematics to recognize that icon."

Of course, the door was locked. Dryce shoved his shoulder against it several times, but it didn't budge. But with the clock counting down, they didn't have time to give up. He took the butt of his blaster and banged it against the door handle, letting out a shout of triumph as the handle gave way and the door broke open. Peyton shoved in ahead of him, looking for their escape.

Dryce didn't see anything that looked like a ship, but a brightly lit empty space in the middle of the room could have been a teleportation hub. Peyton found the control console and started to type madly on one of the keyboards. After thirty seconds she looked up with a smile. "I think I've got it!" she exclaimed.

Before Dryce could respond, the door behind him crashed open and an enemy warrior started shooting.

Chapter Twenty

Peyton got a glimpse of neon yellow skin and a scary looking blaster before she dove for cover, praying to any god she could think of that no damage was done to the teleporter. They had less than five minutes now, and she was not ready to die. She could hear Dryce fighting, blaster shots being exchanged, followed shortly by the sound of fists hitting flesh. The alien who'd come in wasn't wearing armor or a survival suit, so she hoped that meant Dryce was in a better position. She had no idea.

But Peyton couldn't just cower in the corner while Dryce fought this battle for her. She dug a coil of wire out of her bag along with a thin knife that she used to splice it into the teleportation console. She had hoped to use a timer to get them off the ship, but with the alien right there they couldn't risk taking him with them. It was quick work. Oscavian tech was practically as familiar now as what she saw on Earth.

Something heavy bumped against the ground and Peyton risked a glance over the console to see Dryce sitting on top of the alien, a mask of fury on his face as he rained down blows on the man. She ducked back down and tested her makeshift trigger, satisfied when two wires met with a spark and the light on the teleporter hub shimmered.

On the ground the enemy alien groaned. Still alive, but not for long. Peyton sprang up from her position and had to wave one arm around to get Dryce's attention. "Come on," she said, nodding towards the platform. "Leave him there. Let's get out of here."

Dryce's eyes were red and she spotted claws sticking out from his knuckles. The anger on his face made him look more monster than man, but she did not fear him for a moment. She only feared that he was so absorbed by the fight that he would not escape with her. She wasn't leaving him behind.

Dryce looked down at the alien and then back up at her. "He's—"

"This place is going to blow in two minutes," she cut him off. "He's dead already."

"I think—"

"Dryce, if you don't come here right now and teleport away with me we are both going to die. Leave him." She had heard of the focus that warriors could find in battle, a mindset that let them ignore all other threats except exterminating the enemy. But she was not going to let Dryce sacrifice himself for one Wreetan soldier.

He glanced at the alien one more time before scrambling to his feet and joining Peyton. She didn't have a good view of the alien, could only see his feet moving slowly as he curled to his side. Dryce's claws were covered with a viscous yellow liquid that might have been alien blood. Maybe she should have been disgusted, but this was Dryce and he had been protecting her. He could wash the blood off once they were safe.

Peyton glanced up at him and words caught in her throat. She was almost certain that the teleporter would get them home safely. And if not home, at least they would be on Earth. But there was a slight chance, incredibly minute, that they didn't survive the journey. Especially if the ship destructed before their teleport was complete. She wanted to tell him what he meant to her, how he made her feel, but the words wouldn't come out and Peyton couldn't waste another minute trying to save them.

She offered Dryce a smile and took a deep breath before joining two wires together and sending them home.

***

Peyton woke with a gasp, snapping out of the darkness of the teleport and into the light of Earth. She heaved, her lungs aching as they rematerialized millions of kilometers away from where they'd been a second ago. Her fingers tingled and she curled her toes to make sure she still had them all. A head to toe check assured her that everything was there, but her heart still pounded madly as her body decided that *now* was the perfect time to panic about everything that had just happened.

Space.

Self-destruct.

Enemy aliens.

Dryce.

Where was he? Before that panic could double down, she heard a groan and saw her mate lying on the ground at her feet. Crisp brown leaves stuck to his hands, which had just been coated in alien blood. It looked like the sun was setting and he was getting harder to see. But her heart could feel him and the more he moved the more the tension gathering in her chest eased. He might be in a bit of pain from all the fighting, which the teleport only compounded, but he was alive and well enough to make noise.

So where were they?

She crouched down to sit by her mate and take in their surroundings. Her survival suit crinkled around her and made it hard to move. Peyton struggled, curling around to unfasten the hard to reach buttons and cast off the helmet. Only when she sucked in the fresh air of Earth could she breathe easy. Sweat had soaked through her thin shirt underneath and made the air around her chilly, but she didn't care. Not now that she was home. There were lots of trees and the sounds of owls hooting and wind whistling through the branches. They could have been in any of a million places on the planet, but at least she was fairly certain that they *were* on Earth. Brown bark on the trees, green leaves just now turning to reds and yellows and golds, brown dirt, and the scent of nature that had to be unique to the planet.

Holy shit, she'd gone off planet!

She'd been so focused on getting them off of the Oscavian ship that she hadn't taken the time to panic about being separated from eternity by only a thin layer of metal. Now that she thought of it, her hands shook and if someone needed her to rewire another teleporter it wasn't happening unless they could hand her a stiff drink or three to steady her nerves.

No, two emergency teleporter re-wirings was her limit for one day.

After another minute of moaning, Dryce pushed himself up and rubbed his head, cringing as whatever sticky remnants of blood mixed with the dirt on his hands to make a particularly gross version of mud. Then he tipped his head back and got a good look around. "We're alive!" he whooped, as if daring the world to contradict him.

"We're alive," Peyton echoed. She hadn't for a moment let herself believe that they wouldn't get off the ship, but now that they were back on solid ground the realization crashed into her. They'd been two minutes away from dying. If the teleporter hadn't been functioning, they would both be dead now. "Holy shit, we're alive."

She threw herself at Dryce, uncaring of the mess of muck on his hands. The solid presence of his body against her grounded her more than the earth beneath her feet. She could feel his chest rise and fall with every breath, the warm heat of his skin burning through her shirt. She reached for the buttons of his survival suit and had them unfastened in no time, exposing Dryce to the clean air of Earth. The suits were great for offering protections from the dangers of a ship with no functioning life support, but they were bulky on Earth and too much to bear. But she was careful when she folded up the jacket of his suit, mindful that they were in the middle of the woods with no supplies, possibly a very long way from civilization. If worst came to worst, at least the suits would keep them warm.

"Where are we?" Dryce asked. His fingers traced over her spine, the soft movement enough to make her shiver.

She wanted to capture his lips and kiss any questions away, but they had too much to do right now. But the second they had the tiniest scrap of safety she was tearing off his clothes and having her way with him. For days. No, weeks.

Months? She wasn't about to rule that possibility out yet.

Dryce's eyes narrowed slightly. "You've got a look."

"A look?" Peyton did her best to school her expression, banishing thoughts of what she and Dryce would do together once they were safe. "There's no look."

He grinned. "You think I don't know what that look means?" He leaned in and swiped a quick kiss against her lips, the contact fleeting and nowhere close to satisfying.

Peyton leaned in, trying to chase the kiss, but Dryce kept his distance. She pouted and when she realized she was doing it, her face went scarlet. Pouting? Because a man wouldn't kiss her? She was glad they were in the middle of the forest, otherwise she'd launch *herself* back into space.

But Dryce nuzzled his cheek against her, keeping his hands away since they were so dirty. "There's nothing to be ashamed of," he assured her.

"I'm not usually like this," Peyton reasoned. "Especially not in the middle of life or death situations. There are more important things than sex."

"I knew you were thinking about sex!" He laughed, and then pressed close again, the intimate embrace more about staying close than igniting passion. "It makes me glad to hear it, denya. And you've more than shown yourself capable in a dangerous situation."

Her heart flipped when he called her *denya* and she wondered if she'd ever get tired of it. Probably not. She hoped not. "I'm not sure where we are." She'd answered the question he'd asked before she got distracted. "I keyed in the coordinates for one of the central teleporters at my lab with a fallback scenario that dumped us on solid ground within a hundred kilometers of the lab. I can't say I'm shocked we didn't make it back home. Security is ramped up so tightly that there's no way an unsecured port would be allowed open."

"So why did you—" He cut himself off before he could finish the question.

Under other circumstances Peyton might have been offended, but she was still pressed up tight against Dryce and so thankful that they were alive that she didn't have it in her to be upset. "They were the only safe coordinates I could remember off the top of my head."

A loud crack of a branch made them both jump and after she realized what it was Peyton wanted to slump down and laugh, but Dryce held his hand up for silence. His brow furrowed as he peered into the crowding darkness of the world around them and when he looked back to her, he was still tense as hell.

"What is it?" Peyton whispered, her lips practically brushing against his ear.

Dryce took a deep breath and spoke just as quietly. "I don't think we're alone."

Chapter Twenty-One

After a lifetime spent on the barren, icy wasteland that the Detyen Legion had called home for decades, Dryce was surprised to find out how *tired* of forest he was. It went on as far as the eye could see, obstructing his lines of sight and hiding dangers that could cut his denya down before either of them realized they were being hunted.

The wolves had been bad enough, an unexpected threat that could have turned deadly if they hadn't kept their calm. But even then he'd known that they were the ones encroaching on the wolves' territory and the animals had only been defending themselves.

This was something different entirely. He could feel it in his blood.

"That wasn't any soldier who tried to stop us," he told Peyton, his whisper still too loud in the suddenly quiet forest. "I think that was Yormas of Wreet."

Peyton's jaw dropped and he could tell she was about to say something, but Dryce covered her mouth to make sure she wasn't too loud, and then they both winced at the gross mess that was covering his hand. He yanked it away and gave her an apologetic look while Peyton scraped away a bit of the dirt that had transferred.

He didn't need to hear the question to know what she was going to ask. "Yes, *that* Yormas. The one who started this all."

Another branch cracked and they looked into the darkness. Dryce had lost his blaster at some point in the teleport, leaving them with nothing but their wits and his claws for defense. He'd take Peyton's brain over many weapons—after all, she'd just saved them from two impossible situations—but he didn't know if Yormas was armed or what he would do when he found them.

"Could he have followed us through the teleport?" Maybe Dryce was getting ahead of himself. They could only hear whoever was out there, and it was more likely to be a human than anyone else.

But in his soul he knew it wasn't.

Peyton nodded, face pinched. "There might have been enough time. Given the rotation of the Earth and the movement of the ship, it makes sense we would land near each other but not in the same place. Someone could have followed us."

The next sound that came towards them seemed further away, like the danger was moving. Like whoever was out there didn't know where they were.

"I have to see," Dryce said. "I have to know."

Peyton looked ready to object, her face pale with terror, but she closed her eyes, resigned to his decision, and nodded once. "I'll stay put, but if you're not back in a few minutes, I'm raising hell."

Dryce kissed her forehead. "I wouldn't expect anything less, denya."

He melted into the forest and headed towards the sound. Whoever was out there wasn't trying for stealth, sending up Wreetan curses and moaning in pain every time he moved. The language was enough of a hint to satisfy Dryce that the person wasn't human, but he needed to see.

Yormas of Wreet had destroyed Dryce's planet decades before Dryce had been born. He'd stolen his home away for reasons Dryce still didn't quite understand, and doubted he ever would. The kind of evil that had to live in a person to do that was unfathomable.

But what he saw when he got close enough to his quarry to see him almost made Dryce feel pity. Almost. If he'd been anyone else, even an Oscavian or Wreetan soldier who'd been hired to destroy Earth, Dryce would have felt for the broken creature stumbling around in the woods and wailing.

If he'd been anyone else, Dryce might have left him there to survive or perish on his own. But Yormas of Wreet owed a debt to the Detyen people and justice would be served.

A dark temptation tickled at the edge of his conscience. He could take care of it once and for all here, avenge his people for the harm done to them and avenge his new home for the terrors that Yormas had tried to inflict. He'd already injured the man on the ship, and from the way he was listing to one side, he was in no condition to fight. It wouldn't take much. And if there was any sort of last minute escape plan, any plot to save Yormas of Wreet from the consequences of his actions, Dryce could put a stop to that now.

His claws slid out, a silent promise of violence. If he did it now, he wouldn't even feel bad about it. There would be no nightmare, no worrying about whether or not he was the kind of monster who could kill an injured man.

But with a deep breath, Dryce pulled himself back from the edge. His people deserved to make the decision about what happened to Yormas. Whether that meant execution, imprisonment, or something else, he could not make the choice for them.

He had no idea how far away from home they were or what kind of supplies they'd be able to discover. There was something vaguely familiar about these woods, but Dryce didn't trust that instinct. As far as he knew, one wood looked just like another and they could be a hundred kilometers from home or they could be within shouting distance.

Still, he and Peyton would need to lug Yormas back, trussed up like some kind of festive beast. It would add time and suffering to their trek, but it had to be done.

A man more interested in fair play might have walked up to Yormas and challenged him head on, but Dryce didn't know if Yormas was armed, and though the man looked incredibly injured, there was no way to tell if he was faking. He flanked him until he came up behind the tree that Yormas was half-leaning on, moaning lightly as viscous blood oozed out of a wound on his side.

It didn't look good, and there was a decent chance that the man didn't make it all the way back to the SDA base, but Dryce was going to do his best to make sure it happened.

He hooked an arm around Yormas's throat and squeezed, compensating when the man jerked against him. Yormas tried to fight, but by the time he realized what was happening, the struggle was already over.

Using Yormas's own belt, Dryce tied his hands behind his back and checked out the wound on his side. Once he was satisfied that it looked far worse than it actually was, he patted the man down for weapons, kept his blaster for himself, and slung the man over his shoulder.

The walk back to where he'd left Peyton didn't take long, and he had to be making enough noise to warn her of his arrival. But when he got there, the clearing was empty.

Peyton was gone.

***

Peyton meant to stay where she said she would. Really. She even found a comfortable tree to lean against where the bark provided a bit of a cushion for her tired back and it blocked the wind that sent a chill down her spine.

She reasoned that as long as Dryce made it back before full dark, she had no reason to move. That was her plan. Her good intentions lasted for less than five minutes.

First she started pacing. She knew Dryce had a bit of distance to cover and that he could be facing an enemy at the other side. She had to give him time. But that didn't stop her from peering into the darkness and hoping that he appeared.

Another five minutes had her walking a perimeter around the area where she'd said she'd stay. She never lost sight of a tree she'd marked as her home base, so she figured that counted as staying put.

She didn't know how long she would have been able to keep doing that, but when she caught a hint of a familiar smell she couldn't stop herself from exploring. She wasn't completely stupid. She marked the trees as she passed them so she had some semblance of a path back, but the marks got fainter and fainter as she sped up, the smell of pungent fuel speeding her on.

The trees started to look familiar, which was strange in and of itself. She wasn't the outdoorsy type, instead preferring to keep to her lab and all of the amenities that city life provided.

Though, now that she was with Dryce, she figured she'd need to come out of her lab at least a few times a week, if only to keep from having sex on any of the work tables. If they ever got around to actually having sex.

That she could focus on something like this while walking through a forest on the vague hope that she could find a way to get them home told her just how far gone she was.

There was a break in the trees and at first Peyton didn't recognize what she was seeing. It looked like a bomb had gone off. Trees were split in two, broken in half like kindling. The ground had deep gouges torn into it, giant caverns that could have passed for canyons if it wasn't clear that the damage was new.

But it only took another moment to realize that this was the aftermath that she and Dryce had left when they'd been sucked up in the teleport. Yormas's weapon had been so thoroughly entrenched in the Earth that the Earth had broken when it was yanked from it. Her heart broke to see the damage and she trembled to imagine just what could have happened if they hadn't managed to make the weapon disappear.

She'd *known* based on the Detyen history that Yormas was capable of destroying the planet in a single blow, but she hadn't quite wrapped her mind around that fact until right now.

God, if she'd gotten something wrong…

But things were fine now. The bomb was left in pieces on a destructed Oscavian ship. There was no hope of fixing it and smuggling it back onto the planet. And if it hadn't detonated and taken the fleet out with it, then the Earth and Detyen forces were seeing to that right now.

It was done, or it would be soon. The planet was safe.

Now all she and Dryce had to do was find a way home so they could report in and begin the rest of their lives, however that was going to look like. And now that she knew where they were, they at least had a place to start.

"This tastes disgusting, how do you survive on these rations?" she heard a woman's voice whisper through the trees. "At least ours just taste like… beige sludge."

"You make it sound so tempting," a male voice replied.

Peyton knew those voices. She started towards them, crashing through trees and making more racket than a marching band. She didn't care, the team was right there and she and Dryce had their way home.

But when she finally found them, she was met with a blaster in her face followed quickly by a bright flashlight that almost blinded her. Her hands immediately went up and she let out a startled squeak.

"It's me, Peyton. I'm your friend!" She almost babbled more, but the blaster made her bite her tongue.

And then it was lowered, along with the flashlight, and she saw Kayde standing beside Toran with Sierra, Raze, and Dru behind them, all with hands on their weapons.

"Where's Dryce?" Raze demanded. "Where have you been?" The fear in his tone reminded her that Raze was Dryce's brother, and Peyton didn't spend a second offended that they seemed to be more concerned about her mate than her.

"Weren't you guys supposed to leave?" she asked, amazed to find them here. It had been nearly a day since she and Dryce must have disappeared, the teleportation messing with their time. They'd traveled to the far end of the solar system and back, and it looked like their team hadn't gone home, instead opting to camp in the forest for the night.

"Where's Dryce?" Raze repeated, his voice growing more insistent as he took a step forward, his progression only stopped by Sierra's hand on his shoulder.

"He's okay," Peyton assured him, "or he was not too long ago." She'd be going crazy if Ella disappeared, so she could understand where Raze was coming from. "But we think someone followed us here. He went to check it out. I said I'd stay put, but I could—shit, I need to go back."

She turned to go, but Kayde grabbed onto her arm to stop her while Toran spoke. "You're saying there's a hostile out there? You're a civilian, we can't sent you back. Kayde and Raze will go."

"And how do they plan to find where we landed?" Peyton challenged. "I know the way back."

"Landed?" asked Sierra. "What happened to you guys?"

"We'll deal with that later," said Toran. He nodded at Peyton. "Fine, but you stay back. Kayde and Raze will join you and you'll bring Dryce back."

"Of course." Peyton wasn't leaving these woods without her mate.

She was happy to have found the team, would be ecstatic once they were all safely on their way home, but the longer she was separated from Dryce, the more her anxiety began to grow. Had something gone wrong? Was he hurt? Or worse? Bile rose in her throat at the thought and she had to strangle the thought and bury it deep. She'd know if something was wrong with Dryce, she'd feel it in her soul. He said they were bound together by some sort of fated connection. If he was hurt, she'd know.

Please, she prayed, *please let him be okay*.

It wasn't easy to find their way back. Though Peyton had thought she was clearly marking the trees, the cuts were difficult to see in the encroaching darkness. But eventually she recognized a giant flowering bush that she'd passed not long after leaving the spot she'd promised to stay in and it took almost no time after that to find where she and Dryce had landed back on Earth.

And there her mate stood with an injured alien at his feet and a mad look in his eye. They were glowing red and he looked ready to tear the forest down to find her.

Peyton stepped in front of Raze and Kayde, heedless of any danger the injured alien might have posed. Dryce saw them and it took him a moment to realize who they were; his fear for her must have been clouding his judgment. But in a blink they were clutching each other tight, holding on like the world was ending, but nothing could have been farther from the truth.

She forgot they weren't alone until one of the Detyens behind her, she thought it was Raze, asked, "Is that Yormas of Wreet?"

Chapter Twenty-Two

Even though she'd been sitting on the sidelines the entire time this felt like one of the most eventful weeks of Laurel's life. Just hearing it secondhand from Dru was enough to make her head spin, and she couldn't imagine what Dr. Cho had gone through.

"So they accidentally teleported to one of the Oscavian ships?" She shuddered, remembering her own time under Brakley Varrow's care. She still had nightmares about it, though the tight embrace of her mate was enough to keep them at bay most nights. With him gone on his missions this past week, she'd barely slept, mostly snatching moments in catnaps and otherwise living on caffeine and exhaustion. "And she managed to hack an Oscavian teleporter to get rid of a bomb big enough to destroy the planet?" Laurel wanted to meet this woman, not just to thank her for saving the planet, but because she was one of the most impressive people Laurel had heard of.

Dru set a tall glass of soda in front of her and drank from his own bottle of water. She watched his throat work, that luscious purple skin of his moving as the liquid poured down his throat. She didn't hear what he was saying until he waved a hand in front of her face and offered a cheeky grin. "Did you want me to answer your question?"

Not anymore. Laurel's tongue darted out to lick her lips and she caught Dru's eyes tracking the movement, the dark orbs briefly glowing red before settling back to their normal black. The rest of the Detyens who shared the suite with them were off somewhere and Laurel hadn't cared to ask why they'd been granted privacy. The suite was big, but with so many people living there it was also crowded, and stealing a few minutes alone *outside* of their room was a gift she couldn't ignore.

But she did want to know what had happened. They could make the discussion quick.

"Yes, answer, please." She batted her eyelashes at Dru, as if she needed to entice him with feminine wiles, not that she'd ever been able to manage a single wile.

"The basic recap then, is this. They accidentally appeared on the same ship that they teleported the weapon to. The weapon caused some sort of structural damage that sent the ship into self-destruct mode. They found a functioning teleporter and were able to send themselves home, but not before Yormas of Wreet, the man who started this whole mess, found them. He followed them, but Dryce managed to injure and capture him. The Sol Defense Agency and the Detyen Legion made easy work of two Oscavian destroyers, and about half of the fleet has retreated." He spread his hands as if emphasizing a point. "There, satisfied?"

"You manage that pretty well." *Exceptionally* well, actually, though Laurel didn't need to stroke his ego. Despite the danger that had hung over their heads since they'd found one another on Brakley Varrow's ship, Laurel had never felt more happy than when she was around Dru. He settled the wandering places within her and helped her understand how she could find the life she'd been looking for, make something more of herself than what her family had planned for her.

Her mate lifted her up and made her see all the possibilities that the world had to offer.

"I think you could use the reminder." Dru set his bottle down and had her scooped up in his arms before she realized what was happening.

Laurel clung on, and once she was firmly settled in his hold, she leaned in close and sealed her lips over his. Was there a word even better than satisfied? 'Cause the things her mate made her feel surpassed anything she'd ever known before.

***

Dryce was going to murder someone if they didn't let him out of this debrief soon. He'd lost track of the hours some time ago and he had no idea what day it was. His communicator had been confiscated to make sure that nothing had been transmitted through it while he'd been aboard the enemy ship, and the room they had him stashed away in looked more suited for a criminal than a warrior.

He didn't know where Peyton was, though he'd been assured that she was also being debriefed.

Yormas of Wreet had been hauled off to a cell somewhere and Dryce was sure that an army of Detyen warriors and the SDA were debating what to do with him. Dryce would leave them to it. He'd done his part by bringing the man in alive, done more than his part. He just wanted to shower, see his denya, and sleep. The last days had been more eventful than any in his entire life and he could barely keep his eyes open.

Had he slept in the past two days? He couldn't remember.

It was another half hour before a woman in a severe SDA uniform informed him that he was free to go. He jerked out of a half slumber and nodded at her before stumbling his way to the locker room outside of the main training area. He wanted to find his mate and gather her close, but he couldn't do it when he was still covered in all of the filth of the day.

Dryce slathered soap all over himself and stepped under the spray, letting the water do the work for him. It beat down heavy against his head, massaging worn muscles and lulling him into a sense of safety.

He must have nodded off and a harsh hit of cold water startled him. He didn't know how long he'd been standing in the shower, half leaning against the wall, but if the water had run cold, it must have been for a long time. He shut it off and grabbed a towel, drying himself with brutish efficiency, nearly hard enough to bruise.

There was no way that he was in good enough shape to make it home, so he decided to catch a few hours in an on call room before heading out. Though it was just as likely he'd be called back to duty again while the people in charge decided how to settle the threat against them for good.

He stepped outside of the locker room and nearly jumped out of his skin when he spotted Peyton leaning against the wall, arms crossed and clearly waiting. She smiled when she saw him, and bit her lip as if holding back a laugh at his over-exaggerated response.

"You look like you haven't slept in a week." Her own hair was damp and she looked fresh, even if the skin under her eyes was dark from exhaustion. He wondered if she'd managed to grab a nap in the time he'd been interrogated.

"I'm not sure I have," Dryce admitted. "Things have been happening so quickly that I've lost track of time."

His mate nodded. "I know what you mean." She held out a hand. "Want to get out of here?"

Dryce wanted to collapse where he stood and hold his denya in his arms while he did it. "I fear I won't be good company until I've rested."

Peyton wiggled her fingers and didn't stop until he reached out and laced their hands together. "I figured that out. But I've got a nice big bed at home, and escaping the base for a little while will do us both good. Escaping to safety, I mean. No more running through the forests or ending up on enemy spaceships. Just a nice soft mattress and warm blankets. Paradise."

There was no other answer he could give. "Yes."

Her grin grew huge and they made their way out of the SDA compound to where Peyton had a taxi waiting for them. She pushed Dryce into it and followed behind him, leaning against him as they sped off. Dryce tried to stay awake; he had his mate beside him and for the first time in days there was no imminent threat, they could just enjoy being with one another. It didn't seem to matter. His eyes fell closed as they drove through dark streets, and though he didn't slip completely into sleep, he had to be jostled awake when they made it to the building that Peyton called home.

It wasn't much to look at, a squat brick structure that had seem centuries in the city. His glance around the neighborhood showed that it was nice enough, though he didn't see the larger houses he'd viewed when he was sent to talk to influential humans in the government and military.

She led them to the door and let them inside, her moves cautious, like she didn't want to alert someone to her presence. But as soon as the door opened, a light flicked on and a young woman stared at them as if each of them had grown additional heads and tentacles.

"You're home," Peyton told the woman. "I wasn't expecting that."

Dryce wasn't sure if it was the exhaustion or the fact that he'd met so many people, but the woman looked familiar. He hadn't slept with her, that he was certain of. He could remember the faces of his partners, and this woman wasn't one of them. But he was almost certain they'd met before.

"You told me that you were working on some super-secret project and not to get worried, no matter what I heard. I was about twelve hours away from sending the Marines after you," the woman said. "You look like—seriously, Peyton, what's going on."

Peyton took a deep breath before turning to Dryce. "This is my sister Ella. Ella, this is—"

"I know who Dryce NaFeen is," Ella cut her off. "And after all the crap you've given me about aliens, I'm shocked that he's the one you're bringing home.

Peyton gave him a forced smile. "My room is right through there," she pointed down the apartment's single hallway. "First door. I'll be right behind you."

Dryce knew what it was to argue with a sibling. He and Raze had almost torn down buildings when they disagreed. He wanted to stay with his mate and offer her support, but he would only get in the way. Whatever the sisters had to say one another, they wouldn't say it in front of him. So he walked down the hall and found Peyton's room. He slumped down onto the bed and was asleep before he could even begin to hear the whispers of an argument.

***

Peyton was nearly dead on her feet. She'd managed to catch an hour long nap after General Alvarez showed mercy on her, but it wasn't nearly enough to counteract the exhaustion of the past week. She was long past the stage of tiredness where she felt drunk and loopy and now all she felt was a quiet desperation for her bed and the warrior in it.

But from the way Ella was glaring at her, it was going to be a little while until she could slink away. She didn't whimper, but that was mostly because of her older sister survival instincts that told her not to show weakness. Who knew how Ella would exploit that?

"What the fuck, Peyton?" was Ella's opening volley. "For all the shit you've given me about hanging out with aliens, I wouldn't expect you to bring that tomcat home. And you told me you were working! Now you're picking up some guy?"

It flayed Peyton to hear her sister say such things, to see the lack of trust in her eyes. Had their relationship really soured so much in the years since their mother's death? There had been a time when Ella looked at her like she made the stars shine. Now Ella was glaring like she wanted to slap her. "Dryce and I did meet through work," Peyton began, but she could already tell Ella didn't care. She knew how this would go. Ella wouldn't listen to anything Peyton had to say, her mind already made up based on whatever conclusion she'd already imagined.

And the worst part was, Peyton maybe deserved it. She'd spent the last two years judging her sister, silently and not so silently, when she took off for days at a time, hooking up with random people and bringing home a bevy of aliens who were just out for a good time. It hadn't been Peyton's place to judge. Ella was a grown woman, as much of an adult as Peyton, and if she wasn't looking for a long term partner, now or ever, Peyton shouldn't have been giving her the third degree.

For so long, Peyton had been wary of romantic entanglements and unwilling to get involved in purely sexual relationships. She couldn't understand the path Ella had taken and she wasn't willing to learn. And now things had changed. Now Peyton was contemplating emotions more complex than she'd ever thought to experience before, now she was taking chances, both with her work, and her life, and the fate of the planet, that she'd never thought she'd be willing to take before.

But Ella didn't know any of that. Peyton hadn't wanted to worry her sister with news of what could happen to the planet. It had little do with the fact that she was bound by secrecy rules and everything to do with no wanting her sister to worry. But in trying to protect Ella, Peyton had lied to her, hurt her. And there would be no quick and easy fix.

She wanted to tell Ella everything she'd done, or even just let her known that she'd flown in a helicopter, more than once! But Peyton was about to collapse on her feet and she couldn't deal with this now. The planet was saved and the rest of humanity's, and the Cho family's problems, could wait until morning. Or whenever she woke up. She'd long ago lost track of what time it was.

"I haven't slept in forever," Peyton finally said, shrugging out of her jacket and putting her bag down on the couch. "I'll answer anything you want once we're awake, but I can't do this right now."

"*We're?*" Ella called after her. "*We're?*"

But Peyton was walking down the hallway, the conversation falling away in her wake. She smiled when she spotted Dryce collapsed on her bed, and she couldn't remember lying down, but his warmth consumed her and she was asleep and safe for the first time in weeks.

Chapter Twenty-Three

Peyton woke alone. She didn't know when Dryce had slipped out of bed, but it must have been long enough ago that the sheets had lost a good deal of his warmth. She curled up into a ball, trying to banish wakefulness, but now that her mate was no longer by her side and the light streaming in through the windows was assaulting her eyes, she didn't have much choice in the matter. She threw off the comforter and flipped over to see what time it was. A little quick math, well, slow math given that she was still so groggy, told her she'd been asleep for more than fourteen hours. And now that she realized it, her bladder protested and her stomach grumbled.

She slid out of bed and took care of the first issue. She still wore the clothes she'd scavenged at the SDA base. The outfit she'd worn on their mission was a lost cause, covered in dirt, debris, space junk, and enough tears that it looked like someone had clawed it. She'd borrowed what she was wearing from Sierra Alvarez, and it didn't fit exactly right, but last night it had been clean, which was all that Peyton had cared about.

But now she wanted her own clothes. It wasn't anything special, just a pair of pajama pants and an old t-shirt she'd bought at the one hockey game she'd ever attended. Not special, but *hers*. And a sure sign that she wasn't about to run straight at enemy combatants or try to disable their weapons sight unseen. She'd had enough heroics for one lifetime. She'd leave the rest to the warriors and hope that was good enough.

When she stepped out of her room, she didn't see any sign of Ella. Her door was wide open and a glance in her room showed her sister absent. She *did* hear a masculine curse coming from the kitchen and smiled when she saw Dryce standing in front of the food processor, brow furrowed, as if it were the most confusing thing ever invented.

Heat curled low in her belly and wiped out all thoughts of hunger.

Dryce's shirt hung open, exposing his naked chest. When she entered the kitchen she saw that he had on his pants from last night, though they seemed looser, hanging off his hips like one gentle tug could send them falling to the floor.

Oh, she was tempted.

His teal skin gleamed under the kitchen lights and Peyton's hand reached out to touch before she could wonder if it was a good idea. Why the hell wouldn't it be? Ella was gone to parts unknown. They had the place to themselves. And Earth wasn't under imminent threat of destruction. There'd never been a better time.

Peyton slid her arms around Dryce's waist and laid her cheek against his back, the muscle warm under his shirt. "Good morning."

His hand covered hers and he leaned back enough to acknowledge her touch. "We are a bit past morning."

She took a deep breath and inhaled *Dryce*, all masculine and clean and *hers*. Her grip tightened and she couldn't get close enough. She wanted to crawl inside of him and never leave. Or the other way around. It just needed to happen. Now. "I don't care about the time," she said, leaving a trail of kisses over one of his shoulders until she found those dark patches of skin that he called clan markings. She couldn't help herself and nipped at his skin. Dryce startled under her touch, but didn't pull away. She might have whimpered if he did.

She was hot and eager and wanted to haul him back to her room and shut out the rest of the world forever. And though her mind tried to come up with some reason why that wasn't possible, she realized there was nothing keeping that from happening. They were alone and together, what could be better?

She leaned back, keeping her arms clasped around him. "Come on, we can eat later."

Dryce's dark chuckle washed over her, a sinful promise that she planned to make him keep. The memory of the time they'd stolen in the on call room was too tied up in the mission for Peyton to truly enjoy, but now they had time to make new memories, and she was going to hold tight to the opportunity.

But steering Dryce was a bit of a challenge. He was too tall for her to see around, and she couldn't stop herself from plastering kisses against him. That seemed to distract him and he bumped into her walls, sending a photo frame askew and almost knocking over another one. By the time they made it to her room, both of them a little bruised from their journey, they were laughing and seemed to be making a game out of it by some unspoken agreement.

And then they were in her room and Peyton managed to kick the door shut behind them in a feat of dexterity that she doubted she'd be able to manage again. Though she'd never considered herself clumsy, her mind was so focused on the giant warrior in front of her that she was shocked she hadn't yet tripped over her own feet.

Dryce took advantage, twisting in her arms as if she wasn't even touching him and somehow flipping her so she landed with her back on her bed and her mate looming over her, staring at her as if she were a feast and he hadn't eaten in years. Centuries. His eyes shifted from black to red and he sucked in a harsh breath through his mouth. Looking up at him like she was, his teeth looked sharper than a human's and she could see how he held himself like a predator. She'd hate to be his prey. Except for now when there was nothing she wanted more.

The clothes she'd been so happy to slip on earlier were now annoying barriers she wished would just dissolve with a simple thought. If Dryce looked at her any hotter, they'd definitely melt off.

God, he was a work of art. Her eyes clung to him, tracing over the sleek lines of his muscle, her mouth watering with the desperate urge to lick. If her eyes could go red, they would have already, and it wouldn't be out of place. The rest of her was *on fire*.

"When you look at me like that, denya…" Dryce trailed off, swallowing hard and taking a step towards her.

"What?" Peyton rolled onto her side, propping herself up on one arm. She needed to touch him, to feel him deep inside of her, but she was almost as curious to know every thought that was running through his head.

"When you look at me like that I have no idea how we let something as minuscule as the end of the world stop us from doing this earlier." His voice was rough, husky and enticingly masculine.

She shivered as the words washed over her. "Then let's not waste any more time." If she thought too much of the events of the past week she was going to freak out, and no way was she going to let that happen while she was in bed with this amazing man. Alien. Mate. It had sounded unbelievable when he first told her, when she first heard of the concept, but now there was nothing more natural, more right. She needed him beside her, *inside her*, more than she needed her next breath. And if they waited much longer she was going to combust with the wanting. "Take off your shirt," she said. "Hell, take everything off."

If it was even possible, his eyes got redder, but the grin he shot her made her heart flip over, reminding her that Dryce wasn't some dour man who only operated with an intensity that would drive her crazy. He was made of humor and honor and everything she'd always wanted in a partner but never dreamed of having.

She'd never known that she could have Dryce. That she could keep him.

"What are you thinking, denya?" he asked as he slowly pulled off his top, exposing all those hard won muscles.

Peyton's mind went blank as her free hand reached out as if it had a mind of its own. She laid it against his abs and bit her lip to bite back a groan. He was perfection made flesh and if there was any room in her mind for insecurity, she'd be wondering how she could ever measure up. But given the way he was looking at her now, she had nothing to worry about. He looked like he wanted to devour her.

And by god Peyton was going to let him.

But Dryce had asked a question. Her mouth opened and shut a few times as she tried to remember the answer, but nothing came to her. "Pants. Off." Who needed thoughts when she could make demands?

And from the way Dryce jolted as if electricity was arcing through him, he liked it too. Between one blink and the next, he was naked, standing proudly before her like an ancient statue, all of him at attention. Peyton's mouth went dry and the sound that escaped her throat didn't make sense in any language, but from the look Dryce shot her, he understood it just as well.

She'd seen naked men before. Not a lot and not very often, but she knew what to expect when she crawled into bed with somebody. But not when that somebody was Dryce. Everything about him was built to be intimidating. Muscles that could tear buildings down by hand, legs strong enough to run dozens of kilometers without tiring, a broad chest she could cling to and never let got. And that cock. *Damn.*

It didn't look human, not quite, which shouldn't have surprised her, given that he was Detyen. But she hadn't gone searching for information about Detyen mating rituals just because she wanted to climb in bed with him. Okay, she'd checked to make sure they'd be biologically compatible, but nothing more. A girl had to have limits.

It was long and thick, with uniform ridges she wouldn't have expected. Her sex clenched as she wondered what he'd feel like inside of her. It was intimidating to think that she could fit that whole thing into her body, but she didn't think she'd ever been more determined.

She pulled her own shirt off, suddenly too hot and confined by the thin material. If Dryce was going to be naked with her, she wanted to return the favor. For a second, half a second really, a pang of self-consciousness threatened her. He'd seen so many people naked, had been with so many others, that there was no way she could match up to some of his partners. But she couldn't remember the last time he'd mentioned anything about that part of his past, especially when she wasn't the first to bring it up. He didn't need to tell her that he wanted to be with her and no one else. She could see that in the way he looked at her and all the other things he said. He called her mate and she believed him. And she wasn't going to let some niggling thought that ultimately meant nothing ruin this.

Taking off pants while laying down required a lot more wriggling than she'd been prepared for, and by the time she had her pajama bottoms off, Dryce was right in front of her, tempting cock and all. Peyton reached out and wrapped her fingers around it, feeling the velvety heat of him.

How had they managed to wait this long? She never wanted to get out of this bed again.

She rolled her eyes up at him as she stroked his length from base to tip, her thumb brushing over the sensitive end. He groaned and his hips thrust towards her once, as if he couldn't control herself, as if *she* had him completely in her power. It was a heady thought, and something Peyton thought she'd want to explore later.

But not just yet.

A part of her wanted to see him fall to pieces just from her hand, but that was another thing that could go on the list of future plans. She'd need to start a database. Cross referencing was definitely going to be involved. And a whole lot of experimentation.

The scientific method *rocked*.

"Should I fear that look?" Dryce asked. He threaded his fingers through her hair and cradled her head.

Peyton grinned. "No, you're going to learn to love this look," she promised.

"No need to learn." He leaned in and kissed her, obliterating all thoughts, even as her mind spun, wondering about the implications.

His knees trapped her on the bed as he climbed on top of her, not crushing her with his weight, but holding her in place. Peyton let go of his cock, her fingers sliding up his chest until her nails dug into him, hard enough to leave a mark, to show the world, the galaxy, that he belonged to her.

He tasted like home and sin and promise, and as his tongue swept across hers Peyton knew that she'd never had another choice when it came to him. From the second they'd met, the road had led to this moment. Maybe the denya bond had sped things up, but she couldn't imagine a life where she didn't have Dryce NaFeen in her arms, kissing her like it was the only chance he'd ever had, and he had to make it good.

But it wasn't only her mouth he wanted to kiss. She tried to hold him close when he pulled away, but he kissed a path down her chest and further south until he knelt between her spread legs and looked up at her with eyes on fire.

She was going to grow addicted to that look. She could feel it.

And when he set his lips on her, *all* she could do was feel. He used his tongue and his lips and his fingers on her like he'd been training his entire life to bring her pleasure. Peyton babbled at him, encouragement and direction to speed up and then begging him to slow down when she thought she'd come too quickly. Already Dryce seemed to know her body as well as she did, and he toyed with her like she was precious, but not breakable, giving no quarter when she thought she'd had enough but still needed so much more.

Her fingers dug into the sheets hard enough to pull up one corner and slacken everything else around her. Some deranged instinct had her shifting away, even as she thrust herself down on him, his fingers reaching into her and hitting that spot just right so that she saw stars and forgot how to speak.

A million promises and declarations might have flown out of her mouth if she had the ability to form words, but all that existed right then was sensation and Dryce. That was all that ever needed to exist for her universe to be complete.

A twist of his fingers had her crying out, and when he pulled them out of her for a moment she begged for more.

Her sex rippled around him and she was swept away by the pleasure as orgasm crested through her. Peyton panted, her fingers cramping from how tightly they clenched the sheets beside her, but she didn't care. Her mind was clear, blank for the first time in forever, and every muscle melted to putty when Dryce pulled away, showing mercy for the first time.

All she could do was stare at him while he petted her legs, rearranging her like she was his own model to move as he pleased. He wasn't wrong. She would do anything for him in that moment, everything and beg for more. And it might have just been her sex addled brain, but she didn't think so. That explained how sated she was, how her body felt like it could melt away and nothing would be better. But the hot, unfurling emotion in her chest was something bigger than pleasure, something she'd never felt for anyone before. Dryce was in her heart, firmly ensconced and never to leave.

He had his hand on his cock and Peyton licked her lips. She wanted to taste him, wanted to give him the same pleasures that he'd just given to her, but she wasn't sure she could make her body move. Everything felt too perfect.

"Damn," she murmured, unable to come up with anything more profound.

For a moment, Dryce's face scrunched up in confusion. "Is something wrong?" He might have sounded worried if his voice weren't wracked with lust.

"Not a thing." Peyton grinned, almost giggling from how light she felt. She reached out, tugging on his arm until he was on top of her. And then somehow she managed to roll until she had her legs straddling his chest, his thick cock nudging at her entrance. Peyton moaned. This was it, what she'd been waiting for. And she was practically dripping, so hot that she knew she'd come again with almost no stimulation. She needed him inside of her. Now.

And Dryce was right there with her. Their eyes met and they shared a secret, sexy smile, a promise of everything that they could be together. And when his cock breached her entrance, Peyton squeezed her eyes shut and breathed carefully to try and get a hold of herself. She'd already come once, and this next time she wanted to feel Dryce deep within her when it happened again. She wanted to see him lose himself and feel it all the way to her core.

He was thick, even as ready as she was for him; she could feel the stretch as she eased herself down over him. But her body was ready, open and willing to take him all the way to the root. And once he was seated inside, it was like something in her chest clicked into place, reaching from Dryce to her and anchoring them together in a bond almost as physical as the one that connected them in sex.

The denya bond.

She'd known it was real. Known that it was something the two of them felt for one another, but she hadn't realized that she would *feel* it while they were joined together.

She wanted to kiss him, wanted to hug him tight and tell him that she would never let him go. But even more than that, she needed to move, needed the friction that only two bodies could make together in a dance recognized throughout the stars.

And so she did. They found their rhythm, and Peyton set the pace, faster than she thought she'd be able to move in her sex dazed brain. Dryce thrust up into her, fitting her like they'd been meant for one another from their very creation. Sweat popped up on his brow and he grit his teeth as if it was an effort not to blow right then.

His hand reached out and his fingers brushed against where they were joined, rubbing her clit until she was gasping and stuttering, her body losing control as it rippled around her.

With a final few strokes, Dryce buried himself within her and came with a yell, his body arcing up off the bed and exploding with pleasure.

The bond seemed to anchor even further between them and Peyton collapsed to the side, curling up against Dryce and brushing her lips against his shoulder.

"Not bad for the first time," she somehow managed to say with an air of contentment.

Dryce huffed out a satisfied laugh. "Not bad at all, denya."

Chapter Twenty-Four

A day stolen away from the rest of the world had to be paid back, and if Dryce weren't so absolutely sated from the time spent with his denya, he might have been in a sour mood as they drove back to the SDA base. He'd been ordered to report back after he got his rest, and though he hadn't received a call from Sandon or any other member of the Detyen leadership, he knew it would be coming if he didn't show himself.

Peyton had her own duties to see to and a team that was sure to be missing her, so she sat beside him in the taxi as they cut through the streets of Washington, DC. She also sat in his heart, the anchor of the denya bond practically a physical weight he could feel every time he moved. He'd heard his friends speaking of their bonds, but he'd never quite been able to imagine what it would feel like. Until now.

"So what happens next?" Peyton asked. She squeezed his fingers, their hands clasped. If they were within touching distance, they couldn't seem to keep their hands off each other. It would be painful to separate for the day, but they had lives they had to live, and they'd see each other in only a matter of hours. Still, it was probably good for Peyton's sister's sanity that she hadn't come back to the apartment the night before. If seeing Dryce was enough to make her upset, she would be especially angry to know what they'd done on the couch. And the kitchen table.

And the hallway floor.

"Next for what?" They probably needed to have a talk about what their relationship would look like. Would Dryce move in with Peyton? Did she want to move to the suite he shared with his fellow Detyens? How many children would they have? When? Could they make love again right now? He shifted in his seat, trying to get a little relief from the memories that sparked his lust.

"With *that*," she rolled her eyes up and nodded at the ceiling. It took Dryce a moment to realize she was talking about the sky and the Wreetan and Oscavian fleet who'd been attempting to attack them.

News of the skirmish had broken, but no one yet had the full story. And Dryce was certain that the SDA and the Detyen Legion would be doing their best to make sure they never did. Already reports were filtering in that the enemy ships were retreating, their leaders captured. Dryce didn't know if it was true or not, but he'd know once they were back at the base.

"I suppose there will be a trial of some kind," he responded. He'd never dared dream what would happen if they caught the man who destroyed Detya. It had seemed impossible until only a few months ago. And in that time everything had changed. They had answers, they had a home, they had a future, and a small part of Dryce was afraid that he was going to wake up and realize that it was all some fantasy and he'd soon need to make a decision about whether or not he'd sacrifice his soul to further aid his people.

"Is everything alright?" Peyton asked, leaning in closer as if she sensed the dark turn his thoughts had taken.

Dryce kissed her forehead and breathed her scent in deep. "Sometimes it is difficult to believe that everything that has happened in the past few months is real," he admitted.

She didn't offer him platitudes, didn't tell him that she could understand exactly what he was going through. Instead, Peyton held his hand even tighter and leaned flush up against him, physically reminding him that she was there with him, that she wasn't going anywhere. It was more useful than any words she could offer.

And it gave Dryce the strength to imagine what could happen next. "There will be some kind of punishment, probably execution." Even though he knew it was the right thing to turn Yormas of Wreet over, a small part of him still wished that he was the one who'd ended that monster's life. "And there will almost certainly be diplomatic ramifications. But for the first time in a century, we're free to choose our own paths. I don't know that anyone has planned for that."

Peyton snorted at 'diplomatic ramifications.' "*Is* there a policy for when a planet's ambassador tries to commit genocide?"

"I'm a warrior, I'll leave that question to the politicians and lawyers." Someone was surely salivating over that question, but Dryce didn't care enough. He wouldn't stop being a soldier just because his war was over, but for the first time he was starting to wonder what that life would look like outside of those narrow parameters.

The taxi pulled up and Dryce got out to enter his identification code at the first gate, but the power on the scanner didn't seem to be working. He pressed several of the buttons and nothing did anything. A minute later, Peyton appeared by his side.

"Anything wrong?" she asked.

Dryce hit the side of the scanner. "It's not working."

"Hmm." She crouched in front of it and glared, as if the power of her mind was enough to start the thing back up. Then she punched three buttons and the scanner beeped, coming back to life. "That should do it."

Okay, maybe the power of Peyton's mind wasn't a thing to be trifled with. Dryce scanned his ID and they both got back into the taxi, which drove them further onto the base. He made a mental note to let someone know about the malfunctioning scanner, but put it out of his mind.

The base seemed unusually calm, something that only nipped at the back of Dryce's mind until Peyton said something. "Shouldn't there be people?"

She was right. The base was basically a miniature city, and during the day there were always people moving around, walking and driving between buildings, monitoring the perimeter, or simply enjoying the sunny weather. But despite the fact that the sun hung bright in the sky and the temperature was as perfect as could be, there wasn't a body to be seen.

The taxi stopped at their destination and Dryce and Peyton shared a look. Dryce's instincts were screaming at him to tell Peyton to stay in the taxi and go back to her apartment where it would be safe, but one look at her face was enough to convince him that she wasn't going anywhere. And he could be overreacting.

Perhaps everyone on the base had been called inside for some reason. Or maybe the place was closed and he hadn't been notified.

But neither of those options rang true, and as he got out of the taxi, his ears strained to hear anything that would give him a hint about what was going on. Peyton slid out from the other door and closed it quietly. They both watched the taxi pull away, their easiest means of escape quickly retreating, the automated driver having no idea that something could be terribly wrong at the Sol Defense Agency.

The door to the main entrance of the base was closed, as it ought to be, but Dryce couldn't see any movement within the building. He didn't like standing so exposed in the drive, but approaching the building head on seemed to be asking for trouble.

Peyton was looking at him, silently waiting for him to make the call. They understood their roles when it came to danger. He was the protector and he would do his best to make sure his denya was free from harm. But he had to admit, it could be useful to have a tech genius on hand if something went wrong. He trusted

Peyton's skills above anyone else's, having seen just what she could do firsthand.

Dryce turned toward the side of the building where a narrow path led to a place that many people liked to have lunch. It was out of the way, and not easy to spot if someone didn't know what they were looking for. If a stranger was causing trouble with the SDA, they likely wouldn't know about that little hideaway. Of course, if the enemy had come from within, they'd know.

But it was a risk they'd have to take. He and Peyton just needed a place where they could think, could plan, before they did anything else. Dryce's hand was on his blaster, ready to pull it out and twitching at every gust of breeze that blew past them. His instincts knew that something terrible had happened, even if his mind didn't know what.

No one met them on the path, and eerie silence was their only company. He almost wished there were screams. At least then he'd be certain that something was wrong. If the base was under attack, there should have been sirens blaring and some sort of notification on his comm, but all he had was the wind.

And the whispers.

He and Peyton froze on the path when they heard the words floating towards them, too soft to discern their meaning. But they were clearly coming from the lunch area he was leading them to, and with no way to discern their language, Dryce couldn't tell if they were friend or foe.

He pulled out his blaster and nodded for Peyton to keep behind him. He wanted to tell her to hide, but it wouldn't do any good; besides, if there were enemy soldiers around he didn't want to risk her being captured. He'd tear the buildings down brick by brick to get her back if that happened, and damn anyone who got in his way.

They approached with even more caution, but when Dryce caught a flash of bluish green skin and heard quietly murmured Detyen he let out a sigh of relief. He wanted to warn the soldiers that he was coming, but they were being so quiet that he didn't want to give away their position. Instead, he holstered his weapon and walked into the clearing, hands raised in a sign of peace. Peyton walked in behind him.

Sierra, Raze, and Kayde all had weapons raised with the practiced efficiency of those used to battle, but when they realized who he was, they put their weapons back down and their shoulders sagged in relief.

Raze was up in a flash, gathering Dryce in his arms in a tight hug, practically cutting off his air supply. Dryce didn't care, happy to see his brother, happy to see his brother so nakedly full of emotion, so happy that his brother was *safe* for whatever value of safe existed at the moment.

"What's going on?" he asked when Raze finally let him go.

The three looked grim. Raze gave the report. "It seems Yormas anticipated the possibility of capture. A small team of mercenaries infiltrated the holding facility early this morning and freed Yormas and Brakley Varrow. The good news is that their escape vessel was disabled before they managed to take off. However, they've managed to take control of the central building and they have hostages, at least three. One of them is Toran."

Dryce let the information wash over him and pushed his reaction to the news that his friend and fellow warrior was in imminent danger to the side. Toran was a capable man and they'd get him and the rest of the hostages out. "What about the Oscavian warships?"

"That's the other bit of good news," Sierra said. "Intel indicates that most of the Oscavians were mercenaries. With their leaders gone and their paychecks in question, they retreated rather than risk capture. Whatever plan the mercenaries in the building are pulling off, it must not have been widely known. Or they're die hards. Difficult to tell which."

"How are you all outside?" Peyton asked, stepping out from behind him. "Where is everyone else?"

"Toran got a warning to us. We were all training at the time. He told us to get out of the building and stay hidden, that we'd regroup shortly. Dru is still inside somewhere, he's been able to get out a few messages, but they're scrambling the comms and we don't know what's happened since our last check in." Sierra looked worried and determined, and as far as human allies went, she was just who Dryce would ask for, besides his mate, of course.

"How many hostiles?" Three warriors, a human spy, and a scientist weren't exactly a match for an army, but Dryce wasn't going to leave his people to rot, and he certainly wasn't going to let Yormas of Wreet escape justice again.

They settled in at a picnic table while Raze broke it down. Approximately twenty Oscavian mercenaries had managed to infiltrate the building and initiate a lockdown protocol. Most of the Detyen and human forces in the building were locked in rooms or offices, and the weapons cache on the third floor was locked down to prevent anyone from accessing it. Toran and at least two other people were being held by the Oscavians and Dru was somewhere in the building trying to cause as much trouble for the Oscavians without getting caught or putting Toran and the others at risk.

Twenty against five, or six if they counted Dru, weren't odds that Dryce liked, especially not when one of the people involved in the assault was his non-combatant mate.

"We need to end the lockdown." If they could free more warriors from where they were stuck in the building, this would be over.

"The lockdown is the only thing preventing them from stealing a ship and getting out of here," Kayde pointed out. "They either didn't anticipate it when they made it happen, or however they planned to circumvent the security didn't work."

Peyton cleared her throat and all attention turned to her. She offered a small, nervous smile. "I've got an idea."

***

Peyton almost regretted opening her big mouth. She wasn't the warrior, and she certainly wasn't someone who could come up with an idea for how to defeat twenty mercenaries who were holding her friends and colleagues hostage. But it wasn't like anyone else had spoken up, and in this case, she might have information that they didn't.

"I can get us into the building," she said.

Sierra pursed her lips and glared, though not at Peyton. She seemed more frustrated by the situation as a whole, not that Peyton could blame her. "The problem isn't getting in, it's getting in undetected. The room the mercs have taken over gives them access to the security system. They'll see us coming."

"Only if we trigger the security system," Peyton shot back. "I know a way in that isn't alarmed." *That* got everyone's attention. She could tell they were about to demand answers, but that would take time they didn't have. Every second wasted was one where the mercs might decide to start shooting their hostages or something equally destructive. "Once we're inside, I should be able to override some of the door locks without taking down the whole system. We can free our people from wherever they're trapped and end this thing. How does that sound?"

The Detyens and Sierra shared a glance before Dryce grinned at her and put a comforting hand on her shoulder. "Lead the way."

And so Peyton did. The SDA base sprawled over a large swath of land in northern Virginia with dozens of buildings seeming to grow out of the Earth. The mercs had control of the central building and could see who was coming and going, but Peyton had enough understanding of their security systems that she knew they wouldn't be able to see if someone entered another building, not unless they were specifically looking for it. And she doubted they would be.

But she didn't lead the team to the front door of the building where her lab was housed. No, she led them around the side and pointed to a window just out of reach. "The alarm is malfunctioning on that window. I'm not supposed to know that my team disabled it, but the beeping was driving all of us crazy. We were going to report it to base security, but things have been a little busy this week."

If she'd expected a lecture on security protocols, she wasn't going to get one. Raze went first, boosted through the window by Kayde and Dryce. There wouldn't be a convenient ladder on the other side, but Raze handed a chair out the window and they used that to scramble their way through.

The building was deserted and the quiet just as eerie inside as it was out. Now that they were indoors, Raze led the way with Kayde and Sierra behind him. Dryce brought up the rear and Peyton stood in the middle of them all, the only unarmed member of their group. Maybe she needed to learn to shoot a blaster. But that would have to wait until another day.

It felt like eyes were crawling over her as they descended into the tunnel that connected this building to their destination, but Peyton hoped that was just paranoia at the situation. A giant security door barred the hallway in front of them. If anyone input their security code, they'd probably alert the mercs to their presence, and none of them wanted that yet.

But Peyton had just used her mech skills to teleport a bomb off the planet, how much of a challenge could a simple door lock be?

A lot, it turned out. She was cursing up a storm and sweating by the time she managed to figure out how to disengage the lock without alerting the system. She led the others through and they were in the main building.

It should have seemed different from the science building, but it was just as quiet, and if she hadn't known that there were potentially dozens, maybe hundreds, of people locked into rooms and looking for ways out, she would have thought the place abandoned.

The mercs had established their position in the third sub-basement, just outside the holding cells where Yormas of Wreet and Brakley Varrow had been contained. So when they came to a staircase, Peyton and her team headed up towards where the rest of the Detyen Legion and the SDA were waiting for them. It soon became clear that the soldiers and warriors weren't resting idly in their locked rooms.

Booms echoed down the hallway, loud enough to make Peyton jump. The found a door with a bulge of metal sticking out of it and that bulge only grew further as the door rattled with the force of whatever was hitting it from the other end.

"The metal will never give enough to break," Peyton muttered as she got close to the control panel and got to work. Opening the doors wasn't the difficulty, it was making sure that she *only* opened the door that she was working on. The mercs were just as trapped as the Detyen Legion and the SDA soldiers, and Peyton couldn't risk letting them out. If the mercs gained access to the armory or one of the SDA garages and got ahold of a vehicle that could get them off planet, they'd take off with Yormas of Wreet and Brakley Varrow before anyone had a chance to stop them.

So she took her time and was glad that Dryce and the others were there to cover her. Dru finding them almost broke her concentration, but she blocked out whatever he was saying and let herself sink into the tech until it was practically a part of her. It was times like these that she envied cyborgs and the tech that lived within them, though they were so prone to malfunctioning that she'd never consent to cybernetic enhancement.

That was another thought to chase later.

Finally, the lock gave way and a Detyen warrior she didn't recognize stumbled out, his hands clasped around a metal stool that looked ready to collapse in on itself. He stared at her for several seconds, stool raised before he realized that Dryce, Raze, Kayde, Dru, and Sierra were all behind her and ready to help.

"Good to see you, Kendryk," said Raze. "Want to help us take this base back?"

Kendryk nodded. "It would be my pleasure."

Things went faster after that. Peyton didn't know if their progress was hidden from the mercenaries holed up in the bowels of the building, but as the number of soldiers around her grew, she didn't care. Raze took charge, sending soldiers off to different locations to prepare to take the battle to the mercenaries and a spirit of hope seemed to infuse them all. She had dozens of Detyen warriors and human soldiers around her, all working in harmony towards a common goal, and it gave her hope for the future they could have if they worked together.

But first they needed to take care of this final threat.

The armory was the last room they hit, and Peyton's heart was beating fast with excitement. She undid the lock faster than any other, practice making the movements easy. She'd need to report the method she was using to the people in charge, but if they were upset, she'd worry about that tomorrow. Today she'd just be happy that she could get their people free.

Soldiers streamed through the door once she had it opening, making for the racks of blasters and las guns that lined the walls, but Dryce held back and placed a hand on her shoulder, squeezing it lightly.

She offered him a smile. She didn't realize she'd be able to grin under such dire circumstances, but the tide had turned their way and she knew deep in her bones that everything was going to turn out alright. But Dryce didn't look so confident; no, she could read the worry clear as day in his eyes, and she was almost certain of the request he was about to make.

"I want you to go to your lab and lock yourself in," he said, voice somber and shoulders braced for a fight.

But Peyton didn't have any fight left in her, and she had no delusions about her ability to fight. "Is that far enough away to be safe?"

"It's safer than going back outside. Dru's team has taken the security control room back from the two mercs who were guarding it and they've spotted a team of mercs outside just waiting to take anyone out who tries to flee." His eyes were so serious that Peyton wanted to kiss his worries away, but now was certainly not the time.

"Okay. I'll lock down the lab. We've got some hardcore security measures down there. I'll be safe. You bring yourself back to me in one piece." And because he was her mate and he was about to head into battle, Peyton allowed herself one kiss, not quick enough to be anywhere near satisfying, but long enough to gain more than one look from the gathered soldiers.

Peyton took care heading back through the now not quite as deserted halls. Detyens and humans patrolled with determination and from the way they held themselves, she didn't think whatever they had planned would take long. But the mercs still had hostages, and there was no way that her people were going to sacrifice the hostages to take out the mercs. So she could be in for a long and boring wait in the lab.

Better long and boring than full of danger.

She made it to the tunnel that led back to the science building without issue, and once she was through, it was like entering another world. The eerie silence that had plagued the central building fell around her, and when something banged in the distance, Peyton practically jumped out of her skin. She tried to tell herself it was just a door closing or perhaps something to do with the ventilation system, but her steps quickened and her heart beat faster. She just wanted to make it to her lab. To safety.

She was convinced that she'd find an enemy around every corner, but as far as she could tell the building was deserted. Maybe she should have asked to have one of the soldiers escort her, but she didn't think Dryce could spare anyone. She wouldn't be responsible for anyone getting hurt just because she was frightened to walk alone.

The door to her lab came into sight and Peyton breathed a sigh of relief. She pulled open the door before she realized that it should have been locked. Her eyes widened as she saw two hulking Oscavians tearing apart the tables and desks as if they were searching for something.

She tried to back away slowly, before they realized she was there, but one of them looked up and pointed his blaster straight at her.

"You're not going anywhere."

Chapter Twenty-Five

They cleared their way through the building methodically, checking for any wandering mercenaries or traps they'd managed to set. Worry for Peyton flickered at the back of Dryce's mind, but he knew it would be worse if she were with them. She'd be safe in her lab, the real danger lay ahead of him.

If only he could convince his heart of that.

With control of the security room, they could do just about anything they wanted. This whole thing would have been over if it weren't for the fact that the mercenaries had hostages. The mercenaries had disabled the cameras and some of the sensors where they were holed up, so Dryce and his team didn't know exactly what they were walking into. They wouldn't risk a full on assault until they had more information, but time was on their side. The mercs couldn't have much food, and they'd already shut off the water to that part of the building.

It was the mercs outside that worried Dryce the most. The team in the security room couldn't get a firm headcount, and though they'd originally thought it was a small team, the number kept growing, now at about ten mercs, with more possibly in hiding. What they'd thought was a team of twenty now hovered around thirty. And while there were more Detyen warriors and human soldiers, plenty to match them, they couldn't fight an enemy they couldn't see.

"Why didn't they just teleport out?" Dryce asked Raze as they waited for their next move.

"Remember what happened to Varrow last time he tried?" Raze reminded him.

"There's no way to disable that?" A signal scrambler made it impossible to teleport into or out of the SDA base. Varrow had tried using a teleport key that had been embedded in his skin. All the effort had gained him was hours of pain and a lot of blood loss.

"Your girl could, probably. But someone without genius level mechanical knowledge? No chance."

Dryce grinned at hearing Raze call Peyton a genius. She was, it was true. Watching her mind work through a difficult problem was his second favorite thing, his first favorite that didn't involve a bed.

"Keep your mind on the task," Raze chided, but he clamped Dryce on the shoulder. "I'm happy for you." Now was not the time for this conversation, so Dryce only nodded.

Sandon and General Alvarez had been two of the last to be freed from the lockdown. They'd quickly taken charge and when Sandon approached them, Dryce knew that it was almost time for action.

"Security reported an anomaly in the science building. I want you, Raze, and Kendryk to investigate it."

Dryce's heart stopped. He'd sent Peyton there to be safe. "Do we have any more information?" He wanted to grab Sandon by the lapels and demand information about Peyton, but he forced himself to remain still. Assaulting Sandon wouldn't help anything.

"That's what you're going to find out. Now go."

Dryce wanted to take an army; instead he had his brother and Commander Kendryk, a capable soldier, though Dryce had never spent much time with the man. At Sandon's order they moved out and Dryce would have sprinted if he didn't have the two men at his side. He'd resent this assignment if his mate wasn't in danger. Yormas of Wreet was the ancient enemy of his people and Dryce wanted to be one of the team to imprison him, or worse, for good.

But Peyton was out there and possibly at the mercy of the mercenaries who'd come to free Yormas. He'd sacrifice anything to make sure that she was safe.

It was good that Kendryk and Raze were with him, Dryce distantly knew that. They made him use caution when he wanted to run straight into danger, but every minute that ticked by was a minute too long for Peyton to be in danger. They made it to her lab and Dryce knew before they got in the door that there was nothing to find. He could feel the pull of the denya bond deep in his chest. Peyton wasn't here. And she was moving further away quickly.

The lab was a mess, tables overturned and desks askew. They'd been looking for something, but Dryce had no idea what. He was a soldier, not a scientist, and he doubted they would even be able to tell if something was gone without a thorough search.

"It looks like they left abruptly," Kendryk said, his tone so detached that Dryce wanted to punch him. The man wasn't soulless; he still had all of his emotions, but from his tone, he might as well have been. "Either they heard Dr. Cho and fled, or she stumbled upon them and they took her with them."

"This is my denya you're talking about," Dryce bit out. "Show some respect." He took a step towards Kendryk, but Raze held him back.

"He's being respectful," Raze told him with a warning look. "We will find her. Never fear."

"And if it was Sierra?" The walls were closing in around him and he needed to run, needed to hit something. If Raze didn't get out of his way, he would do.

"I'm on your side, brother, but watch what you say." They stared at each other for a charged moment before Dryce gave a minute nod. Now was not the time to upset Raze, and he couldn't alienate Kendryk either, not if he wanted to get his mate back.

"I can sense her," he told them. "And she had no reason to leave this room, not unless they took her. Even if she were hiding, I'm sure she would have found a place to stay put. They have her."

He waited for one of the men to argue. It was conjecture, but Dryce was certain of it to the root of his soul. Peyton wasn't the type to take unnecessary risks. She'd only be on the move if the mercenaries had her or if they were chasing her. Either way, if they found her, they'd find their targets.

They left the lab as it was and Dryce followed the tug in his chest, taking them out into the courtyard behind the building where they were forced to slow down. Enemy mercs were outside somewhere and moving without caution would get them dead.

The pulse of the denya bond grew stronger and Dryce wanted to run towards it, but he tamped down that urge with all the discipline that had been enshrined in him over his entire life. But the closer they got, the harder it was to fight the urge, and when he heard a feminine cry, nothing could have stopped him from running towards it.

They found Peyton under guard of three mercenaries, two of them with their blasters pointed at her. A bruise was blooming on her cheek and she'd been forced down onto her knees next to the door of what Dryce vaguely recalled was one of the auxiliary hangars.

The fight ended before it began, with Raze and Kendryk each taking out a merc with their blasters. Dryce launched himself at the third, taking him to the ground and pummeling him with fists and claws until his hands were covered with Oscavian blood and the beast within him was satisfied that his mate was safe. Bloodlust pounded in his veins, an unquenchable thirst for vengeance for any who dared to lay a hand on Peyton.

And it was only Peyton's hand that could pull him back from that edge. She murmured soothing words into his ear and placed her hands on his shoulders. "It's okay," she said. "I'm safe now. You saved me."

He wanted to kiss her. Wanted to take her to bed and prove to both of them that they were alive and nothing would harm them again. But there were still mercenaries running around, and no place was safe for Peyton until they were taken care of.

He looked up to find Raze and Kendryk waiting patiently for him to recover from his outburst. There was no judgment in Raze's eyes, though he couldn't expect Kendryk to understand. "Let's finish this," he said. He was ready to take his mate home, but first it was time to take care of the enemy once and for all.

***

Peyton expected a final showdown to be more exciting. Not that she actually *wanted* any more excitement in her life. One unplanned expedition to an enemy spaceship was more than enough. But as the standoff ticked over into the third hour, Peyton was actually a little, well, *bored*. She was sitting in the middle of a freaking hostage crisis, her face still smarted from the bruise that regen gel was rapidly healing, and she knew she'd have nightmares for years to come of seeing those mercenaries in her lab.

If Dryce hadn't shown up when he had…

No, she didn't want to think about it. She'd been able to stall them for long enough, sure that Dryce, or someone, would find her. They'd wanted her to open the door to the auxiliary hangar where they would be able to find a vehicle to get them off the planet. Whether they had a plan for breaking Yormas of Wreet and Brakley Varrow out, Peyton hadn't determined, and she hadn't cared that much. All she'd wanted to do was survive.

Now all she wanted was to go home. Or at least to take a nap, but she didn't think that would go over well. She'd always thought that a battle would be a pulse pounding, edge of your seat affair that was over as quickly as it started. And maybe a battle would be, but that wasn't right now.

The mercenaries had freed Yormas and Varrow, but they were trapped in the third basement of the central building. The Detyens and humans had cut off all avenues of escape, but they hadn't yet advanced. The mercenaries were holding Toran and two others, a Detyen and a human that Peyton didn't know, captive. Once they moved against the mercs, the hostages would almost certainly be killed.

Peyton kept hearing snatches of plans for extraction, but there was no way in or out, not any stealthy way, at least. If this were a media show, someone would be able to climb through a conveniently placed vent and the day would be saved.

"What are we seeing? Has our status changed?" General Alvarez asked one of the Detyens over the comms to the security room. Even after working at the SDA for so long, it was hard to believe that she was standing near such a legend. He'd singlehandedly saved Mumbai from an alien attack.

With a jolt, Peyton realized that someday people might say her name with as much reverence as they spoke of the general. She shuddered at the thought and prayed that her part in this whole mess never got out. She wasn't some big hero, she'd just been doing her job. It wasn't *that* difficult to reprogram a freaking teleporter.

"No change, sir," the person in the control room answered back.

She heard a muttered curse. Peyton felt invisible. After recovering her from the mercs, there'd been no question about Peyton staying with the large group of armed soldiers who could ensure she was safe. And though she wished Dryce could be by her side, she understood that he had work to do. But everyone was so focused on the problem in front of themselves that they may as well have been looking through her anytime a head turned her way. For her part, she was trying to stay as quiet as possible.

"Unless you can get me into a locked room without using a door, this ends one of two ways: the mercs turn on their bosses in exchange for leniency, or everyone ends up dead. Do you see another option?" She wasn't sure who Alvarez was talking to, but his words echoed into her head.

Get me into a locked room without using a door.

"We need a distraction." Peyton didn't realize that she'd spoken until every eye in the office turned to her.

Alvarez stared at her expectantly but Peyton wasn't sure what else he wanted. "Yes, a distraction would be useful."

"Dad," Sierra said in warning tone. Peyton hadn't realized that she was in the room until she spoke. It was crowded enough to be stifling and sweat made Peyton's clothes cling.

She didn't have an idea for a distraction, but Alvarez looked ready to tear into the next person who crossed his path, and she'd accidentally put herself in his sights. She scrambled for anything she could give him, immediately dismissing half a dozen ideas. If there was already something in the room they could use, they would have thought of it. From what she'd heard, they had a visual feed into the room, but the audio was being scrambled and none of the hostages had their communicators or any other way to maintain contact.

They needed to get something into the room, and they couldn't get it through the doors. "Why don't we use the teleport?" She had teleportation on the brain, but it had worked in her favor so far, so why not keep at it?

"Teleportation doesn't work on the base," someone said, as if she had no idea how the tech work.

But Peyton dismissed them with the smallest wave. She pushed out of her seat and started to pace. There was a small sliver of space by the wall where she was able to manage it. "Teleportation is only scrambled if you're trying to get off the base. We've used them on base before since it's the easiest way to move some of the larger equipment." And sandwiches when the lab staff was too lazy to walk all the way to the mess hall, but Peyton didn't say that part out loud. "We can't move people, the scrambler is strong enough to interrupt any signal that large, but we could get a weapon to our people. Or..." what else would be useful, Peyton wasn't sure, "a smoke bomb?"

"Why didn't you suggest this two hours ago?" one of the Detyens demanded, rounding on her. She had long dark hair and blue skin, but Peyton didn't have a name to go with the face.

She'd met more Detyens in the past week than she had in the entire time since they'd come to Earth.

"That doesn't matter." Alvarez stared at her like he could see deep into her soul. "What do you need?"

***

Dryce wasn't in the front line to go through the door once they had the signal, but he was still close enough that the astringent smell of smoke tickled his nostrils and sent a shot of pride through him. The first and second groups of soldiers wore gas masks to keep the soporific drugs from clouding their senses.

Once they called the all clear and had Yormas of Wreet, Brakley Varrow, and the rest of the mercenary team secured, the team in the security station engaged the HVAC system to clear the gas from the bomb. By the time Dryce and his team entered, there was nothing more than the faint scent of smoke in the air with a hint of something sickly sweet he wouldn't have been able to name if he didn't know what had happened.

His mate was not a woman to be messed with.

It hadn't taken long once Peyton realized she could rig a teleporter to transport something small into the room where the mercenaries had holed up. And when Sierra suggested that they use a drug that many Sol Intelligence Officers were familiar with to knock out the enemy, it hadn't taken long.

Dryce was satisfied to see Yormas of Wreet and Brakley Varrow returned to their cells, both left in manacles so as not to risk another escape. They'd be moved to separate holding facilities once the base was secure, but until then, they'd be under twenty-four hour guard and heightened surveillance.

Seeing Toran lying unconscious wasn't something he'd like to repeat, but a medic was already tending to him, and he'd wake with little more than a headache in a few hours.

The next hours were spent routing out any lingering mercenaries and securing the base. Dryce wanted to steal a minute away with his denya, but by the time he managed to get near her, she was ensconced in conversation with several Detyens and a few humans and was so focused she didn't notice him.

Day wore on into night and he was commanded to catch a few hours of sleep before he dropped, but Dryce knew he'd been more rested than anyone who'd been caught on base when the whole ordeal began so he switched off a ship with a young Detyen who practically cried in relief when she was told she could grab a few hours of sleep.

When morning came around again, Dryce admitted defeat and crawled into one of the on call rooms, startling awake sometime later when a warm body burrowed in next to his, but it was Peyton, and he slung his arm around her and relaxed as they both fell into sleep once more.

She was gone in the morning, but when he was summoned to the largest conference room the building had to offer, he saw her sitting near General Alvarez and a few other humans. She gave him a tired smile and he took a seat beside Toran, who looked much better.

"Exciting day?" Dryce asked with a smirk. "I heard you passed out at the end of it."

Toran glared at him. "Some of us were called from our beds earlier than others, and neither I nor my mate would like to be reminded of it."

Dryce bit back a laugh and schooled his face into a more sober expression when Sandon stood and began to speak. The debrief was long and tedious, even if hearing everything Sandon and General Alvarez imparted sent waves of relief through Dryce.

The Oscavian mercenaries who hadn't been involved in the attempt to liberate Yormas of Wreet and Brakley Varrow were confirmed to have left the solar system. The Oscavian Empire disclaimed all knowledge of the attack and already had diplomats on the way to soothe ruffled human feathers. Yormas of Wreet would be given to the Detyens according to their laws, and Brakley Varrow would be tried in human court.

All signs indicated that the weapon that Peyton had teleported off the planet was the only one of its kind, and with Yormas in custody, they didn't fear another one being produced. He'd guarded the secret so closely for a century that it was difficult for anyone to believe that he'd shared it widely. And if he had, they'd deal with that later.

Hours passed and Dryce had to pinch himself to stay awake a time or two. But when it was done, he stood up and looked around the room. There were a few soulless warriors at the meeting, their expressions as blank as always, but every other Detyen in the room seemed to be thrumming with energy, no matter how tired they were.

It was hope, Dryce realized. The kind of hope they hadn't dared dream about since the destruction of their planet. They had a new home on Earth now, and their people's greatest enemy had been defeated. He was no longer a shadow. And though they didn't yet know why he'd targeted Detya or eventually turned his sights to Earth, Dryce hoped that they'd one day figure it out.

But, the second realization came to him on the heels of the first: if they didn't, it would be okay. He couldn't hurt them anymore, and he was completely at Detyen mercy. His motivations didn't matter. The Detyen race lived on, and they'd continue to flourish, especially now that they'd discovered their compatibility with humans.

Peyton slid an arm around him, having weaved and dodged her way through the crowd to find her way to his side, just where she belonged. "Ready to go home?" she asked, head tilted up and a smile on her face.

Dryce kissed her. He couldn't go another moment without it. When he pulled away, he heard a few mutters from the people around them, but nothing mattered except the woman in his arms. "I'm ready," he said. "Let's go."

Chapter Twenty-Six

One Month Later

"Tell your stupid mate that if he doesn't pick up his damn towels I'm going to throw all his clothes in the incinerator!" Ella pounded on the door of their bedroom, her tone harsh enough to say she meant business.

Peyton considered it an improvement. Ella had barely spoken to her or Dryce during the first week after he moved in. Now she glared and threatened, but she seemed to be warming up to the hulking Detyen presence in their life.

And Peyton was still shivering with the memory of what Dryce had done to her *after* leaving the towels on the floor that she wasn't in the mood to chastise him. She cuddled up next to him, laying her head in the crook of his arm that seemed to be made for her. "Stupid mate, pick up your damn towels next time," she murmured, all sleepy and sated. Really, it seemed unfair that so many people didn't have mates. She'd never been more sexually or emotionally satisfied in her life.

Dryce let out a very male grunt, though he didn't say anything. Of course, he took a few minutes to recover his ability to speak after making love, something she hadn't realized immediately. Mostly because he drove her so crazy with lust that it took her almost as much time to recover her own wits.

Of course, whenever Ella suspected them of getting nasty (Ella's words), she made a face like a disgusted teenager and fled to her room, as if she'd never taken someone else to bed before. But Peyton knew she'd sprung this change rather suddenly on her sister, so as long as they were making some kind of progress, she'd call it a win.

Things couldn't have been going better with her and Dryce over the last month. Sure, there were hiccups, like when they'd run into one of his former lovers who seemed to think they might be up for a threesome and wouldn't take no for an answer until Peyton threatened to call the cops. The reminder of his past wasn't exactly welcome, but he'd never made Peyton feel anything less than wanted, and she was beginning to be thankful for all those past lovers.

After all, she was the one benefiting from all that practice. And *damn*, practice did make perfect when it came to Dryce and sex.

Work had been weird at first. People on the SDA base looked at her with awe when they realized who she was, and sometimes fear. Others had taken to calling her 'teleporter girl' which made her want to insist that she knew about way more than just teleporters. Dryce cautioned her to let it go. She'd saved the world, people were going to talk.

Thankfully her name hadn't been leaked to the public at large, and since the story of Earth's near miss still wasn't widely known, she didn't need to fear becoming as famous as General Remington Alvarez. And she hoped it stayed that way.

She'd gotten to know the human mates of the Detyen warriors over the past month, and a few of Quinn's friends who were survivors that had been rescued by Sierra and her team. It was a big, convoluted group, but they'd accepted Peyton into their ranks without blinking an eye. And none of them called her teleporter girl.

"What are we doing today?" she asked. They both had the day off work, and she'd been showing Dryce as much of the city as she could manage, though it turned out, he'd explored plenty on his own. They each had their favorite places to share and were coming up with ideas for future vacations. They were building a life together, one idea at a time.

"Raze wants us all to meet at their place. Says he has an announcement." Dryce idly played with her hair, neither of them making much effort to move.

Peyton had an inkling that she knew what that announcement was, but she kept her mouth shut. She hadn't wanted to say anything, in case they were keeping it a secret for a reason, but if there was a little human/Detyen hybrid on the way, Peyton couldn't wait to know more.

"Then I guess I have to shower *again*." She grinned as she said it, pushing herself up and swinging her legs out of the bed.

Dryce tugged on her wrist until she sprawled over him so he could steal a kiss. "I could join you." He offered with a wolfish grin.

Peyton rolled away and held up a hand to ward him off. "Then I'd need *another* shower and my sister is scandalized enough, you sex fiend."

Dryce tipped his head back and laughed. "Everything I do, I do for my denya."

Her heart flipped over and she bent down to kiss him again. "I love you."

He stole another kiss before letting her go. "I love you, too. Now go get ready. Raze will go mad if we're late."

So Peyton did as she was told, ignoring Ella's eyeroll as she took her second shower of that morning. Earth was safe, she had her mate with her, and annoying her little sister was just one of life's tiny pleasures. Peyton couldn't imagine anything better.

***

Also by Kate Rudolph

Sci-Fi Romance

Snowed in with the Alien Beast

Crashed

Mated on the Moon

Red and the Wolf

Mated to the Alien

Ruwen

Tyral

Stoan

Cyborg

Krayter

Kayleb

Detyen Warriors

Soulless

Ruthless

Heartless

Faultless

Endless

Paranormal Romance

Marked

Bear in Mind

Alpha's Mercy

Gemma's Mate

The Mate Bundle

The Alpha Heist

Entangled with the Thief

In the Alpha's Bed

Find more by Kate Rudolph at
www.katerudolph.net

<u>About Kate Rudolph</u>

Kate Rudolph is an ex-derby girl who lives in Indiana. She loves writing about kick butt heroines and the steamy heroes who love them. She's been devouring romance novels since she was too young to be reading them and had to hide her books so no one would take them away. She couldn't imagine a better job in this world than writing romances and sharing them with her fellow readers.

If you enjoyed this story, please consider leaving a review.

Are you a STARR HUNTRESS?

Do you love to read sci fi romance about strong, independent women and the sexy alien males who love them?

Starr Huntress is a coalition of the brightest Starrs in romance banding together to explore uncharted territories.

If you like your men horny- maybe literally- and you're equal opportunity skin color-because who doesn't love a guy with blue or green skin?- then join us as we dive into swashbuckling space adventure, timeless romance, and lush alien landscapes.

http://eepurl.com/b_NJyr

Printed in Great Britain
by Amazon